NIGHTFALL

NIGHTFALL

THE FAIRHAVEN CHRONICLES BOOK FOUR

MARTHA CARR

MICHAEL ANDERLE

LMBPN Publishing
PMB 196, 2540 South Maryland Pkwy
Las Vegas, NV 89109

First US edition, December 2017
Version 1.11 January 2020
Print ISBN: 978-1-64202-801-0

Thanks to the JIT Readers

John Ashmore
Larry Omans
Paul Westman
Erik Cushman
Thomas Ogden
Joshua Ahles
Tim Bischoff

If I've missed anyone, please let me know!

Editor
Lynne Stiegler

DEDICATIONS

From Martha

*To everyone who still believes in magic and all the possibilities
that holds. To all the readers who make this ride so much fun.
And to all the readers just like me who create wonder, big and
small, every day.*

From Michael

*To Family, Friends and
Those Who Love
To Read.
May We All Enjoy Grace
To Live The Life We Are
Called.*

CHAPTER ONE

Victoria rested her elbows on the edge of the safe house's windowsill and peeked through a gap in the pair of tattered curtains. Styx slept on her shoulder, his head leaning against her neck as she stood guard. A tilted fence framed an overgrown yard and separated the weeds from the pockmarked street. Half a dozen mansions lined the road, but a candle burned only in one other window at the end of the lane.

This was a forgotten street, for the most part—a once-great collection of homes that now mainly served squatters—and for that reason it made the perfect hideout. Victoria hated to hide, especially from Luak, but unfortunately she had no choice at the moment.

Around her neck, the diamond pendant her parents had left her glowed brilliantly. The necklace hadn't stopped glowing since she returned home from Atlantis.

She lifted it over her head and stuffed it in a pocket. *Why bother?*

Victoria was constantly in danger. As long as Luak

lived, she would always be a breath away from death's door.

The steady march of boots on pavement caught her attention, and she craned her neck to get a better view through the tattered curtain without jostling it. No one could know she was here, but she still wanted to know what happened outside these walls.

A troop of mercenaries carrying torches walked in step down the street. They all wore the same black uniforms and marched five abreast, staring straight ahead as if they were a disciplined military and not swords for hire.

"Assholes," she muttered under her breath.

"Another march?" someone asked from the doorway.

Victoria yelped and spun on her heel, summoning her sword as she faced the stranger. Styx fell off her shoulder and hovered in the air barely a foot from the ground, his tiny wings startled to life.

"Whoa, chill out," Audrey said from the hallway, hands in the air as she backed away.

"Jesus," Victoria said, palm on her chest as the rush of adrenaline subsided. The sword in her hand disappeared and she cracked her neck to relieve the tension.

Styx grumbled and shot into the hallway, probably in search of another place to snooze.

"You okay?"

"Yeah, I guess." Victoria peeked again at the marching soldiers as a voice muffled by the glass called for an about-face. They stopped mid-step and turned back the way they had come.

"Things have really deteriorated since we went to

Lochrose," Audrey said, glancing through another rip in the curtains.

"No kidding."

"We lost the west tunnels, too," Audrey said with a nod to the hallway.

"Damn it." Victoria rubbed her temples. The tunnels beneath Fairhaven had always been a safe space to go undetected, but she was slowly losing access to them thanks to Luak's guards. Every time she and her friends went in, it seemed like a new stretch had a regular patrol.

Audrey slumped against the wall and kicked the floorboard. "How does he even have an army this big? He's just one elf."

"Money. Those are all mercenaries. Whoever his boss is, they're loaded."

"What are we going to do, Victoria? We can't fight all of them. The army gets bigger every day."

Victoria set her hands on an exposed section of windowsill and huffed. Bit by bit, Luak was squeezing her out of hiding. He was building up to something. Something big. Something bad.

Victoria had to strike first, but she needed resources and the right timing.

Lost in thought, she barely felt the sill crack under her grip. She pulled herself out of her dark thoughts to find an imprint of her hand in the wood, with jagged splinters sticking up every which way.

"You're going to kick ass in Berserk," Audrey said with a chuckle, eyes on the imprint.

That, at least, got Victoria to laugh. Her newfound strength was incredible. She could lift ogres now, and she couldn't wait to use it on the Berserk field. She figured she probably violated all sorts of rules just by existing, but she didn't care in the slightest.

No one got between her and her favorite game.

"When this is over we should restart the games as soon as possible," she said.

"Yeah, like a tournament or something."

"Winner gets Luak's head as a trophy. We can get it bronzed." She chuckled.

Audrey grimaced. "You're fucking dark, you know that?"

Victoria shrugged. Berserk would reignite the hope that Luak had slowly squeezed out of everyone in the city, and she was certain there were more than a few who would enjoy that grand prize.

She peeked through a hole in the curtain again, craning her neck to watch the mercenary army as it rounded a bend, blissfully unaware that they had just walked right by her.

Hopefully "blissfully unaware" would be a running theme with Luak, but she knew better.

Across the street, the charred remnants of a once-great mansion was evidence that he was doing everything he could to flush her out. He had ordered it burned about two days after she had returned. The roof had caved in during the blaze, and fire had leaked from every window while smoke had billowed to the cavern ceiling far above.

Now a sign was posted out front.

Victoria Brie is a menace. Report sightings to the castle guard.

She snorted in disgust. Calling the mercenaries "the

castle guard" was the final straw. It was evidence that Luak had far more control over the city and the monarchy than she had originally thought.

This was the final chapter in her war with Luak, and it was up to her to see to it that Fairhaven had a happy ending.

Since she had returned to Fairhaven Victoria hadn't had many moments to herself. Her hideout had to accommodate an ever-growing list of refugees, including Bertha and Edgar. The rooms were filling, and she almost always passed someone in the tense and silent halls.

It was better that way, since it kept her from losing herself to thoughts of the crumbling city around her.

It also meant she could train.

With the increase in guards in the Fairhaven tunnels, Victoria, Fyrn, and Audrey had fewer and fewer caverns in which they could practice. Each time they used a cavern they crossed it off, because it was inevitable that they had left evidence in their wake.

Usually in the form of crushed boulders.

"Again!" Fyrn shouted.

Today they had found a cavern filled with boulders with which she and Audrey could practice their aim and self-control. The little pixie hovered nearby, watching from a distance as Victoria practiced. She took a deep breath, clearing her head as she prepared to obey her mentor's command.

She adjusted the shield in her left hand, grip tightening

on the metal that protected her from Fyrn's attacks. It was the largest shield she could muster, and it barely weighed anything, or so she perceived now.

In her other hand she held her largest sword, which was almost taller than her. She couldn't believe how effortless it all was—that she could hold something this massive and not feel even the slightest bit of strain in her shoulders and back.

The bear figurine was turning out to be the absolute perfect second Rhazdon artifact for her. It complemented her first in every way possible…except for its ghost.

There was no nice way to put it: Elle was a fucking psycho.

Shoving the thought aside, Victoria focused on the nearest boulder. As commanded, she lifted her sword over her head and aimed for its center, and with one deft swing she sliced it perfectly in two. It cracked open like a dessert with a surprise filling: a collection of glittering amethyst crystals filled the center.

"Sweet, another geode," Audrey said.

Victoria scanned the large cavern and the other two dozen boulders she had cut open. All of them were filled with various crystals, but none were as beautiful as the amethyst in front of her.

"We can decorate the house with your practice objects," Audrey said with a snicker.

Victoria chuckled. "My geodes beat your fried pieces of target paper. Can't really put one of those on the fridge."

Audrey shrugged. "I don't worry about aesthetics. I just like destroying things."

"Can't argue with that."

They had been training for roughly two hours now, Fyrn drifting between them as they practiced their new skills. Audrey had shifted into a witch and now walked around blasting paper targets to smithereens. She also concealed the tiara on her head with almost effortless ease, walking around and breathing normally as if it hadn't been utter torture just a few short weeks ago.

It seemed as though with every day that passed Audrey gained better mastery over the dark magic merged with her forehead.

Thank freaking goodness, because Victoria would need all the help she could get when she finally faced off with Luak.

"How do you feel?" Fyrn asked, with a wary glance at her shield.

"Great, actually," Victoria said with a grin.

Audrey lifted one delicate eyebrow. "Seriously? We've been at this for ages. I just want to pass out."

Victoria shrugged. "I feel fine. You can take a break, though."

Audrey wrinkled her nose. "Is that a challenge, woman?"

"Maybe," Victoria said with a grin.

Since she had a new Rhazdon Artifact to master, Victoria had begun with the easiest skill to access: her strength. Now, for the first time since fusing with her dagger, she was able to wield both her shield and her sword simultaneously. It was simple, as if she had been doing it her entire life.

She was now able to either duck or block every blast of

painful energy Fyrn threw her and she didn't tire, even if they trained for eight hours straight.

But that wasn't all her new Rhazdon artifact could do.

Strength in body, mind, and heart. It was so vague, and the possibilities seemed endless. Though she didn't understand how to access it, Fyrn had told her she now possessed immense physical strength, almost limitless emotional control, and enhanced intelligence.

This was a truly powerful Rhazdon artifact, one she had no doubt many men had coveted over the centuries.

The trouble was *accessing* all that power.

"There you go again, daydreaming!" Fyrn shot another blast of fiery energy at her.

With a graceful spin she avoided the bolt, but it crackled against the wall behind her and a surge of adrenaline burned in her core.

"Maybe if you threw me a challenge I wouldn't have time to lose myself in thought," she said with a mischievous smile.

He frowned, which she thought was freaking hilarious.

Audrey laughed. "My, my, my! Did Victoria finally get under the great Fyrn Folly's skin?"

"No," he snapped quickly. *Too* quickly.

"Oh, I definitely did." Victoria chuckled. In the past she would have snapped at him for the sneak attack or complained about exhaustion, but not today—not since she had fused with the bear figurine.

The exhaustion and frustration that usually accompanied her training sessions was gone, replaced by cool composure. She felt calm, in control, and ready for the fight.

She just didn't know why or how to control it at all.

With the dagger, she had struggled and then overcome. She had fought for every skill she now possessed, but with the bear figurine, her new power was as natural as breathing.

Truth be told, that scared her. Her new abilities felt impermanent, like she could lose this new sense of calm and control at any moment. And if she didn't know how to control these gifts, they might fail her when she needed them most.

Regardless of how much or how little control she had over the bear figurine's power, people would try to kill her for it, Luak among them. But every one of them would fail.

In the meantime, she had to protect the ever-shrinking population of Fairhaven.

Victoria easily dodged another seven blows from Fyrn. With her body moving instinctively, she turned her attention to Audrey. "Did you find out what happened to that missing aristocratic family of elves? Did they just leave the city?"

"Oh, you have time to banter now, too?" Fyrn said, voice tense and annoyed. He shot a volley of light at her, which she dodged easily.

"Guess so," she said with a wink.

He fumed.

Audrey lifted her practice wand and shot a blast of light at the wall. "That rich family you asked me to tail? The bankers?"

"Yeah."

"Will you— Ugh." Fyrn shot a twelve-bolt combo, and the last shot came close to hitting Victoria's shoulder. It flew past, but while it sizzled a few threads on her shirt it left her otherwise unscathed.

Audrey shrugged, ignoring the angry old wizard. "That family disappeared overnight, so I thought at first that they had simply escaped the city. They certainly had the means to do so. After all, they were the second richest family after the king."

Victoria faltered at the memory of the king's corpse in the pile of bodies back in Lochrose. Though she had never liked him, he hadn't deserved to die broken and alone.

Fyrn shot another bolt of energy at her, and she quelled her sorrow quickly in order to roll out of the way.

And just like that, she was back in the game. Her sadness over the king's death simmered below the surface, but she could focus on the task at hand while allowing herself to feel.

Sweet.

"So the banking family escaped?" Victoria asked. It would be a disappointment if they had, since their wealth and influence would have helped fund an attack on the palace.

Victoria didn't want anything to do with mercenaries. They could be bought, and their loyalties changed like the wind. She needed real fighters who would lay down their lives for their cause, not strangers who had never set foot in this city.

But influence—now *that* couldn't be bought. The bankers had had connections, friends in high places both in and outside of Fairhaven. They would have been useful.

"Sadly, no," Audrey said. She shot another bolt of energy at the ceiling, and a stalactite dropped. Victoria rolled out of the way as the massive rock smashed to pieces, shaking the ground beneath them. Fyrn, however, simply waved his hand, and a dome of energy surrounded him. The flying debris bounced off its surface.

"What happened to them, then?" Victoria asked.

"The parents and elder son are gone. Just…gone. The younger son, who's about our age, insists they're traveling, but I saw mercenaries going in and out of his house, and he's a jumpy little fellow. Always looks nervous. I'm pretty sure he's the last surviving member."

"That's the third wealthy family to disappear since Luak overthrew the throne," Fyrn said with a frustrated sigh. He leaned on his staff, apparently taking a break from fuming and grumbling to himself to join the conversation.

"It seems like that asshole has the same idea we do," Victoria said, leaning on her sword.

Luak was already wealthy, and now he had even more money to spend on his mercenaries.

Yippee.

"How are we going to beat him, Fyrn?" Audrey asked.

Fyrn nodded toward Victoria. "With the one thing he doesn't have."

"Enormous boobs?" Audrey asked with a wicked grin.

Victoria chucked a rock at her, but Audrey ducked out of the way, still laughing. The rock hit the wall so hard it splintered.

Oops. Victoria would have to be more careful when it came to playfully hitting her friends. With her newfound strength, she might break them.

"Real power," Fyrn said with an eye roll. "And a secret weapon."

Victoria eyed him warily. "Are you referring to—"

"You'll see," he interrupted, putting his finger over her lips to silence her.

Victoria trusted her mentor, but she sure as hell didn't like the sound of that.

CHAPTER TWO

After several more hours of training, Victoria was barely winded.

Mostly she felt pissed that her training had been interrupted by what could only be called utter nonsense.

"For the last time, Shiloh," she snapped, "you cannot call Elle a 'psychotic idiot.'"

The ghost stared at her with a lifted eyebrow as though baffled by the statement. "But she *is*."

She let out a string of curse words under her breath. Audrey, meanwhile, laughed so hard she doubled over. Styx held his tiny stomach, squeaking with mirth. Fyrn wasn't much help, since even he could barely suppress a smile.

"It's not my fault she's an insane little girl," Shiloh said matter-of-factly.

"*Little!*" a young girl's shrill voice echoed through the cavern, though no one could see her.

Elle.

Victoria sighed and leaned on her sword, rubbing her temples. "Guys, I can't have you bickering while I fight. You're distracting, and you might get me hurt."

"How awful," Shiloh said, his voice lacking any hint of remorse.

Victoria frowned, eyes narrowing as she studied the ghost. He was tied to her dagger Artifact, and she had thought he had warmed up to her in the tunnels of Lochrose, even going so far as to warn them of coming danger. He had quite possibly saved their lives, and even though she didn't particularly enjoy his company, it wasn't like him to want her dead. "What's going on, Shiloh?"

"She's obnoxious and invades my space."

"You're a ghost. You don't *have* personal space."

He paused his examination of his fingers to glare at her. "I have few joys in this world, Victoria. Solitude is hardly too much to ask."

She raised one hand in gentle surrender. "Fair enough. Elle?"

"Yes?" Her sheepish voice echoed through the cavern.

"Please leave Shiloh alone."

"But I'm *BORED*!" the disembodied voice screamed.

Victoria lifted one eyebrow and leaned toward Fyrn. "Can ghosts get bored?"

Fyrn shrugged. "I didn't think so, but perhaps I was wrong."

"Or perhaps she's batshit-insane," Shiloh offered.

Victoria, Audrey, and Fyrn all turned their heads to stare at the ghost elf, who never lifted his gaze from his fingernails.

"Elle, come here please," Victoria said, ignoring her other ghost.

There was a pause. "Do I have to?"

Victoria let out an exasperated sigh, but Audrey stifled laughter. "You're like a mom, V."

"Shut up, you."

That just made Audrey laugh harder, and this time Fyrn joined in.

"Fyrn, this is serious," Victoria said, gesturing to Shiloh. "What if they bicker during a real fight?"

Fyrn nodded, his expression sobering. "You're right, Victoria, but you'll have to figure out what to do about this. I'm afraid I know nothing of the way Rhazdon ghosts interact with each other."

"We don't," Shiloh said, gloomily.

"Well, you're going to have to learn how," Victoria snapped at him.

He frowned and disappeared, and the lingering echo of Elle's voice faded as well. Victoria sighed and tried to piece together what they'd been fighting about.

A flicker of inspiration hovered just out of reach in the back of her mind. It was an incredible sensation, as though someone were handing her the answer on a silver platter... if only she could reach it.

She furrowed her brow, diving deeper toward the elusive thought, but it vanished.

With a sigh, she wished away the sword and shook out her hands to keep her blood pumping. "That was odd."

"What?" Audrey asked.

Victoria frowned again. "I'm not sure. I asked myself a

question, and it was as though the answer was suddenly there in my mind, just out of reach."

Fyrn nodded, a small but undeniably proud smile on his face. "You're already accessing more of the bear figurine's power, no doubt."

"What do you mean?"

"It offers you enhanced intelligence, which means better pattern recognition and deductive abilities. Even without full information you'll instinctively know the answers to the questions most of us don't even think to ask. Pursue that flicker of thought, Victoria. Don't let it fade."

She nodded. "I'll try."

"Good. For now, I'm going to retire to do more research. Perhaps my fairies or I can find information on how to manage the warring personalities of multiple Rhazdon ghosts."

"Good luck with that," Audrey muttered.

Victoria shot Audrey an annoyed look.

Her friend just shrugged. "What? You've seen the way those two bicker. Fyrn will need every ounce of luck he has to figure this out."

Victoria frowned. She hated to admit it, but Audrey was right. If those two bickered during a battle with Luak, Victoria wouldn't get out of it alive.

Fyrn let out a slow groan as he sat back in his office chair. His back cracked from hours of leaning forward as he read through his various tomes, and a sliver of relief snaked down his spine.

His boot kicked over a pile of books, and a plume of dust mushroomed into the air. He eyed the toppled volumes, wondering if Victoria had a point about hiring a maid.

Nah.

He tapped his finger on the armrest, eyes slipping out of focus as he stared at the door. As the gemstone sky darkened outside, several enchanted candles flickered to life in the sconces on the wall and in the hallway, and long shadows stretched behind the various piles of research and papers throughout the room. Each pile was a reminder for an unfinished project, and the layers of dust told him which was more urgent.

Victoria, of course, had interrupted most of his plans.

Bickering ghosts. Newfound powers. Enhanced intelligence. She had much on her plate, and yet she always remained focused on the ultimate goal: freeing Fairhaven by killing Luak.

Her time would come. In fact, he wondered how much longer she would even need his help.

His shoulders drooped slightly. One day she would surpass him. It had already begun, and her growing powers made it inevitable. Her glares at the castle had gotten grimmer, so it seemed that day would come sooner than he had originally thought.

A draft swept past him and the office's candles were snuffed with a hiss. His eyes narrowed as he eyed the dark sconces warily.

He didn't *get* drafts in this house.

It had dimmed to near pitch-black outside as the night progressed, and Fyrn had lit only the few candles in the hallway sconce to cast a dim light into the office. With a second gust of air from nowhere, those went out as well.

In the darkness, Fyrn listened.

Nothing.

No footsteps. No breathing. Not a peep from the hallway, living room, or kitchen.

He stood and snapped his fingers to summon his staff, and it sprang from its place in the corner and nestled into his palm as he waited for something to happen.

Someone meant to unsettle him by invading his home. This was an attack, though it had yet to turn bloody.

It would.

Whoever was orchestrating this had access to powerful magic if they were able to get past his spelled perimeter without him having known. He or she would need to have access to the highest-quality potions and mastery of the magical arts to rival his own. Few had such potential, and the only one he knew of who was still in Fairhaven was loyal to Victoria Brie.

But Diesel would never invade his home.

This was someone else. Someone deadly, and they weren't here for tea.

An arrow whizzed past his ear, and he instinctively tilted his head to avoid it. It landed with a *thunk* in the wall behind him.

After that shot, all hell broke loose.

Bolts of magic blew his precious piles of books to dust and scrap paper and blinded him, the searing slashes illuminating the darkness like flashes of lightning. He cast a magical shield, summoning the energy deep in his core to ensure it would be strong enough to block the volley of spells tearing his home to pieces.

The bolts ricocheted off the magical dome protecting him, burning holes in every surface as they rebounded. Battle cries drowned the sizzling hiss of magical energy tearing through paint and wood. Fyrn grimaced and strained as the onslaught slowly wore down the shield protecting him.

Hand crackling with blue light, he released a torrent of spells at his still-unseen attackers in the hallway. The light shot out like a single bolt of electricity, then the edges splintered off in erratic arcs that stung any living creature they could find.

By the spells' light he could finally see into his hallway, or rather, what *used* to be his hallway.

A chunk of the wall had collapsed in the attack, revealing at least eight elves kneeling as they pressed themselves against the remaining surface. A few ears poked out of the ruins, and the rest were scrambling to find cover.

Damn.

This was worse than he had imagined. If this many were in the hall, more would be waiting in the other rooms and outside.

His house would not survive this attack.

"This will be fun," he grumbled under his breath.

He launched several more blistering attacks into the hallway to distract them as he inched toward the secret door in his bookcase. If he could get to the tunnels, he could outrun them.

If forced he could probably kill them all, as long as they had only a handful of wizards aiding their attack. However, he preferred to keep his house in one piece, and he doubted they cared as much about his possessions as he did.

A bolt of light from the hallway shattered his bookcase and tomes tumbled to the floor. He waved his staff and the books flew across the room, giving him a moment of cover.

Now for a proper exit.

The crystal on the top of his staff glowed white, filling the room with a light as bright as the sun. Several of the mercenary elves covered their eyes with their hands and temporarily stopped attacking.

"Perhaps we can resume this another time, gentlemen," Fyrn said. He lifted his staff and struck the ground with it, and a ripple of light radiated outward. A gust of wind surrounded him, kicking up the loose pages in the room, and the paper circled him like a tornado. After a sharp crack the entire house trembled, and a burst of energy knocked out the remaining wall in the hallway.

Mercenaries screamed and fell backward. Bones cracked. Bricks and wood buried several of the soldiers, and they would have a hell of a job escaping.

That should buy him time.

With a smirk, Fyrn slipped through the secret door and shut it quickly behind him.

He trotted as fast as an old man could through the tunnels, his feet taking him toward Bertha's old shop. She had run back to get a few things, but he feared she would be next on the hitlist. He would need to warn the ogre before heading to Victoria's safehouse.

It seemed Luak had changed the game.

"Where are you off to, wizard?" a deep voice asked.

Fyrn slowed, his back stiffening as he scanned the dark tunnels. Nothing lurked there, and he would have sensed someone running after him. His grip on his staff tightened.

From the darkest shadow a white grin emerged, and seconds later a familiar Light Elf's face followed.

"Luak," Fyrn said, tensing.

Luak nodded. "Bravo for making quick work of those idiots. They were supposed to wait for you to leave your office to avoid this very scenario, but I suppose they got bored. You do sit still for quite a long time."

Fyrn scanned the darkness, wondering if Luak had been foolish enough to come alone. He stood a chance against the elf in honest combat.

But this was Luak. He didn't do *honest*.

Luak sneered and opened his mouth to say something else, but Fyrn knew how this would go. Banter, banter, banter, and then surprise attack from behind.

Not today.

Fyrn shot a bolt of red-hot light from the tip of his staff without giving Luak the chance to finish his thought and it hit the elf square in the chest, shooting him backward into the wall. He cracked his head against a jutting stone, grunting from the blow, and a massive crack ran toward the ceiling as the force of Luak's impact split the rock wall in two.

Without giving the elf a moment of reprieve, Fyrn followed the bolt with a volley of blows. Every attack hit something on Luak's body and he grunted and groaned with every blow, body trembling from the force of the magic slowly cooking him. Smoke streamed from the elf's shirt and ears.

This was the only way Fyrn could win. Fyrn was immensely powerful, but Luak had a deadly Rhazdon Artifact on his side, or maybe more than one. If Luak ever dealt him a blow it would be over.

"Enough!" the elf snapped. A tornado of fire erupted from his palms and scorched the cave, and the blast of heat knocked Fyrn to his back. He rolled and got back to his feet.

The elf walked through the inferno as though it didn't faze him, and considering the elf's Rhazdon Artifact, it probably didn't.

"I had hoped we could speak like civilized men," Luak said coldly, "but it seems like you need some sense knocked into you first."

He swung at Fyrn too fast to see, and his fist connected with Fyrn's temple. The old wizard grunted and shuffled backward, head spinning as he tried to catch his balance. He blindly shot several bursts of blistering light toward Luak, not sure of his aim, and Luak grunted in pain.

Good. One of his blows had hit.

They cast at each other for several minutes, their deadly dance slowing as two of the most powerful men in Fairhaven dueled to the death.

At least, such was Fyrn's intention.

He could not retreat. He would either kill Luak or die trying, and with every passing second it became less clear what the outcome would be.

Luak scowled, the lines in his face deepening as the combatants retreated farther into the dark tunnels. He kicked Fyrn in the chest, knocking the wizard onto his back. Fyrn grunted, gasping for air as he tried to get back on his feet, but he didn't get the chance.

Luak's hand glowed blue, casting dim light in the tunnel around them. Beetles scurried along the walls, scampering away from the sudden illumination, and Fyrn lifted his staff to block whatever attack was headed his way.

"No," Luak said simply. He spread his fingers, and Fyrn's staff began to tremble violently in his hand. Fyrn summoned his magic to quell the shaking, focusing all his energy and power into the crystal at the tip of the staff, but even his painfully tight grip couldn't keep it still.

"What are you doing to..." Fyrn gritted his teeth, losing his train of thought as he fought the violent tremors.

He couldn't let go of his staff or he would lose.

"Let's see how strong you are without your precious magic," Luak said, his eyes glowing the same color as his hand.

The shuddering staff began to hum, and with a pang of terror Fyrn realized too late what was happening.

Beneath his fingers, the staff snapped.

The painful *crack* echoed through the tunnel like thunder, shaking Fyrn to his core, and the shattered remnants of his staff fell to the ground.

He now held only the top portion in his hand, and as he watched the light within the crystal faded. As the magic disappeared, his body groaned, his muscles weakened, his legs ached, his back curved, and he fell to his knees.

"That's better," Luak said, breathing heavily. "I thought I

would never get a clear shot. You're a quick draw, Fyrn Folly, but you're no match for me."

Fyrn tried to stand—he would not die on his knees—but the battle had zapped nearly all his energy. Instead, he glared at the Light Elf before him with all the composure of someone about to deal a fatal blow. "I refuse to bow to you, Luak."

"You're doing a pretty good job of it," the elf said, with a nod at Fyrn's slumped shoulders.

Fyrn tried again to stand, but his legs would not hold him. He fell hard on his palms, grimacing as pain shot up his arms.

He sighed, more disappointed with himself than afraid. He'd had a full life, one of adventure and discovery, and if this was his time he would go without complaint. His only regret was leaving Victoria when she needed him most.

"Where's Victoria?" Luak asked, hands behind his back as he circled his prey.

"Somewhere safe."

Luak pressed his boot against Fyrn's back and something snapped. He yelled in agony, reflexively summoning magic he didn't have to heal the wound. Jaw tense, he slumped and grabbed the crystal that had once topped his staff, wishing with all his might he could run Luak through with a sword right now.

But he couldn't. Even the great Fyrn Folly could be defeated.

"Where?" Luak asked, his voice a low growl.

"If you want to kill me, get on with it. You won't get anything out of me."

Luak laughed, and the dark sound sent a chill down

Fyrn's spine. It was too confident. If Fyrn didn't know better, he would think Luak already knew the answer. The elf's boots came into view as he finished circling, and Fyrn glared up at him.

"I don't want you dead, wizard," Luak said with a sneer. "At least…not yet."

CHAPTER THREE

Victoria quirked an eyebrow, a small smile playing on her lips as she eyed the ogre in front of her. "You want me to do what now?"

"Tackle me," Edgar said, gesturing for her to come closer.

They stood on a makeshift Berserk field not far from the safehouse in one of the farthest and least-known tunnels Fairhaven had to offer. Even revolutionaries needed to let off steam, and Victoria had been running around the jagged field for the last hour with Edgar and three of his brothers.

Apparently Bertha's whole family was *huge*.

Victoria set one hand on her hip and chuckled as she tried to understand just what Edgar wanted from her. "But why do you want to wrestle *me*? I've seen you on the Berserk field. You're a beast."

"I am, and most would be crushed beneath me." The other ogres rolled their eyes and shouted at him to shut up, but he hushed them with a wave of his hand and pointed at

Victoria. "You, however, are different. With your new Rhazdon Artifact, I doubt I'll be able to so much as touch you."

He nodded toward the bear figurine on her abdomen beneath her blouse and she stiffened, but her powers were no secret among the ever-growing population of the safehouse. Given everything she had inadvertently crushed—from windowsills to pots and pans—there was no keeping a secret this big.

And surprisingly, no one cared.

There were no riots. No angry expressions. No fear. After everything she had endured, everything she had sacrificed for Fairhaven, they trusted her completely.

These were *her* people, the only ones who truly loved her as she was.

She hung her head in mock defeat and waved him forward. "Fine. Show me what you've got, Edgar."

A mischievous grin spread across his face, and he shook out his hands to prepare himself. His eyes narrowed on her shoulders, just as they did when he picked a mark to tackle in practice.

Any other time, Victoria might have gulped with nerves. Any sane human would have been terrified of the four-hundred-pound ogre about to barrel toward her.

But Victoria wasn't quite human anymore.

She took a short step back and tilted her shoulders as she prepared to intercept him. She had watched Edgar tackle at least a hundred people, and he almost always favored his right side. Since he was one of the largest ogres on the field, that usually didn't matter—anyone in his way ended up on their back, seeing stars.

Not today.

He charged, the rocky ground shaking beneath him as he raced toward her.

Victoria held her position, lazily watching him approach. As predicted he leaned to the right, preparing to hook her arm and throw her over his head.

Nope.

She grinned and pivoted at the last second, looping her thin arm around his waist and hoisting him over her head as if he weighed nothing. He yelled as he sailed over her and hit the ground with a thud. The impact shook rocks loose from the ceiling, and a few shattered against the cave floor.

The three other ogres on the Berserk field hooted, shouting at him in the ogre language Victoria still needed to learn. She didn't know what they were saying, but her best guess was something along the lines of, *"That skinny chick just whupped your ass!"*

Edgar, however, said nothing.

For a second he didn't move, and Victoria was worried she had hurt him. She leaned forward, trying to get a glimpse of his face. "Edgar? You okay, buddy?"

With a sudden intake of air, Edgar burst out laughing and rolled onto his back. He held his sides as tears poured down his face. He tried to speak, but just laughed harder.

A trickle of relief relaxed her shoulders, and she laughed along with him. The other three ogres joined in, and soon there was a queue of ogres waiting to be flipped over her head like rag dolls.

She wiped a happy tear from her eye and shook her head. Freaking ogres, man. They were weird as hell.

CHAPTER FOUR

Armed with a bag of pot pies and the stubbornness of a mule, Victoria headed to Fyrn's to help him with his research. Styx sat on her shoulder, greedy little eyes fixed on the bag in her hand. If she didn't watch him, he would eat all her food.

As she meandered through the underground tunnels, she bit into one of the small pies and wondered if books could solve her Luak problem, or if she would just end up bickering with her mentor before heading home.

With him, it was always a tossup. Regardless, she plodded along the less-used tunnels, wondering when the "castle guard," as Luak had referred to the mercenaries, would take over this section of the Fairhaven underground as well.

Plain and simple, time was running out. She would have to face Luak soon, and she couldn't wait to skewer the bastard.

Audrey pressed her back against an alley wall, sticking to the shadows as a pair of elves in black uniforms passed the exit onto the street. They muttered something beneath their breath, gazes focused on each other.

If they were supposed to be patrolling the streets, they were too busy gossiping to do a decent job of it.

Time to infiltrate the enemy.

Are you sure this is wise? the koi asked gently.

Audrey scanned the alley for a reflective surface in which to see the ghost that accompanied her Atlantean Artifact, but none were available.

Fine. She would just talk to herself like a crazy person.

"We need intel, and I can't stand being cooped up anymore," she said softly to ensure no one overheard her.

Victoria would be most upset.

"That's why I'm not going to tell her unless we find out something useful."

But to walk with the enemy is dangerous. If Luak discovers you...

"He won't. I won't even see him. I'm just trying to get information from his captains and the grunts in the field. I need to know where they're planning to look for us, and the low-level soldiers will at least have rumors to go on."

The koi paused. *I suppose so. Be careful, Master.*

Audrey lost her train of thought, still not used to the title her little water spirit had given her. She wasn't anyone's master.

You are mine, the koi corrected.

She sighed. *Fine.*

With a shimmer along her skin, Audrey shifted into the form of a Light Elf. Her spine stretched, making her a good foot taller, and her facial features rearranged themselves. She hadn't yet figured out how to change into a man—the idea made her smirk—and the koi didn't seem to know anything about that either, but each race had unique features, and except for the witch form she was almost unrecognizable when she shifted.

Her nose sharpened to a point, and her ears poked through her silky hair. Starting at the tips of her hair, the color bled from black to blonde. Her fingers thinned. Everything about the elves was slender and elegant, and part of her wished she had been able to pick up some of the Light Elves' magic ability. So far it didn't make a lick of sense, though. She would figure it out in time, but until they deposed Luak she had to focus on what she could do well.

She glanced down at her familiar clothes, which were now straining on her tall form.

Hmm. She didn't have any clothes that would work for an elf.

Push your limits, the koi suggested in its melodic voice.

"Thanks, that's not cryptic or anything," she muttered softly.

Change your clothes.

"I can do that?"

My previous master was able to. Try.

Audrey squeezed her eyes shut, careful to slink further into the shadows so she could experiment without being seen.

A tingling hum reverberated through her body as she imagined the black uniform the mercenaries wore on patrol, from the loose-fitting pants tucked into the military boots to the black button-down blouse embroidered with a fiery crest that could only be Luak's coat of arms.

She wiped a bead of sweat off her brow as the pressure in her core built, but she held her focus. Within seconds the pressure released, and she let out a slow sigh.

She glanced down to find the black uniform exactly as she had envisioned it, except for the hems being slightly uneven and the shirt a little too large. It dwarfed her thin frame like a tent, and she frowned with disappointment.

You will perfect this ability in time, the koi said softly in her mind. *For now, celebrate the success.*

A small smile spread over Audrey's lips. "Thanks."

After a tentative peek to ensure no one was watching, the disguised Audrey swaggered into the road as if she owned it. A few castle guards passed her, but none of them gave her the time of day—except for one leering orc who seemed unable to keep his gaze off her ass.

She couldn't linger. There weren't many women in Luak's mercenary army, and she could only imagine what those girls endured behind closed doors.

Scratch that. She didn't want to imagine it.

A group of mercenaries meandered toward the castle entrance, which had been thrown open to reveal a bare tunnel. When she and Victoria had visited the castle, they had gone through a different entrance. Aside from a few sconces lighting the way, nothing adorned the walls. This entry seemed threadbare, likely meant for the people the king didn't care about impressing—like the guards.

Two soldiers scanned every face that passed. Her heart beat faster as she neared them, and she wiped her sweaty hands on her pants to quell her nerves.

If they pulled her aside, she might not be able to convince them she belonged. She had to act like the rest of these assholes—tough, rude, and curt.

Shouldn't be too hard. She suppressed a smile at her little joke.

A few of the mercenaries ahead of her nodded deferentially to both sentries. When one of the guards settled his gaze on her face, she mimicked the soldiers ahead of her and nodded once.

He frowned, his eyes running over her body once before he nodded back and turned his attention to the orc behind her.

Thank Christ, oh my God. She let out a slow breath, careful not to show her relief on her face.

The swarm of soldiers ambled along a dimly lit corridor wide enough for ten men to march through shoulder to shoulder. At the end of the hall two massive doors sat open with fire pits on either side, their leaping flames reaching the ceiling. Inside, more elves and orcs in black uniforms congregated around a raised platform in the middle of the room.

She squared her shoulders, hoping this little plan of hers would work. Time to gather some intel.

To escape as much scrutiny and attention as possible, Audrey pushed against the flood of bodies in order to circle back and stand behind the door. The murmur of dozens of overlapping voices filled the crowded room as she waited.

Finally, after about five minutes of anxiously scanning the passing faces and scowling at anyone who made eye contact, Audrey perked up. A massive orc pushed his way through the crowd toward the platform, his black armor shimmering in the firelight and the glow from the dozens of sconces along the room's walls.

"Shut up!" he roared as he stepped onto the platform.

The room quickly obeyed, the murmur fading to near-silence as he waited for them to stop talking.

"We have new orders from the king," he said, raising one hand. "Our hunt for the Rhazdon host is priority number one. Continue arresting anyone who tries to leave the city, and escort anyone who enters the city to the castle regardless of which entrance they use."

Get to the good stuff. Audrey wasn't feeling particularly patient, and the longer she was here the more men looked her way.

Damn, she wished she could figure out how to shift into a dude. She would blend in so much better.

"As for the host," the orc continued, pacing on the platform with his hands behind his back, "we suspect she is in the elvish sector. Double your patrols in this area."

Ha, idiot! She and Victoria were miles from the elvish sector. At least they had bad intel. That would buy them time.

The orc continued for another ten minutes, detailing which of the tunnels they were to expand their patrols into this week. Audrey repeated the important information silently to herself to ensure she remembered it, eager to slip out at the first opportunity.

The army was looking in the wrong part of the city, so she and Victoria were in luck...for now.

Deep in the tunnels underneath Fairhaven Victoria held her breath, her eyes wide as she pressed herself against a boulder. In the shadows, she and Styx were hopefully hidden from the seven Light Elves who marched down the tunnel.

A second later, four more elves stepped through the secret door that led to Fyrn's house.

"This is bad," she muttered to herself.

Fyrn would never have allowed Luak's army into his house, and she hadn't seen him on her way here. Hopefully he was back in the safehouse, but a sinking feeling in her gut warned her that wasn't the case.

This had to be Luak's doing, and there was no chance Fyrn had come out of this without injury. She grabbed a rock off the ground and crumbled the stone to dust in her anger.

If Luak had killed Fyrn, she would ensure every second of her enemy's death was as painful and prolonged as possible.

Fyrn was missing, his house had been overrun, and Luak may have very well just scored a point against her in this brewing war.

***

Fyrn groaned as he lay with his face pressed against a damp stone floor.

He blinked himself awake, body sore and screaming for a healing spell, and pushed upright, leaning against a stone wall as he scanned the darkness around him.

The steady drip of water echoed in a vast space, and a

thin ray of light bled through a crack in the ceiling at least thirty feet above him. It illuminated the gloomy outline of his cell, complete with the iron bars he knew would be enchanted against any charms or spells he could throw at them.

Could have thrown at them if he had his staff, anyway. Without it he had no power.

He sighed and squeezed his eyes shut, disgusted with himself. He had allowed Luak to destroy his staff—the artifact and relic that had not only given him immense power throughout the years, but which had also prolonged his life for more years than any one wizard should ever have had.

Without it, he would not be long for this world.

He could repair it, but only if he escaped both the cell and whatever Luak had planned for him. And without magic or help, there was little hope of that happening.

"He finally awakens," a familiar voice said from the darkness.

Fyrn's jaw tensed and he stubbornly squared his shoulders to hide his pain. "Where is my staff, Luak?"

The elf emerged from the cell's shadows, and Fyrn wondered how long he had been waiting to make the dramatic entrance.

"Oh, this?" the elf lifted the crystal that had once sat at the tip of Fyrn's staff.

Fyrn tried not to show his relief—at least the elf hadn't destroyed it yet. Instead, Fyrn frowned. "It's rather cruel to destroy an old man's walking stick."

Luak chuckled. "I'll get you another one if you behave."

"And if I don't?"

Luak lifted the crystal into the light, admiring its facets

as the ray splintered through it. "I'll keep this as a souvenir of the day I destroyed the late great Fyrn Folly."

A flicker of hope ignited in the back of Fyrn's mind as he realized Luak had no idea what he was holding or the power the crystal could give him when paired with the right artifact.

Thank goodness.

Fyrn feigned boredom despite his racing pulse. "Any other threats you'd like to make before we get started?"

"Just one."

"And that is?"

"If you don't tell me where Victoria is and how to defeat her, I will ensure you live only long enough to see me burn her alive. You will watch as I destroy what you created, and then I will destroy what's left of you."

"I don't—"

"You know exactly what I'm talking about," Luak interrupted. "You've hidden your connection to her rather well, all things considered, but I know you've been training her. I know you've been guiding her, building her, refining her until she will be able to defeat me. But she won't, because you're going to tell me everything I need to know to kill her."

Fyrn forced a laugh. "We can be honest here, Luak. There's not a thing you can say or do to make me utter a word against her."

Luak sneered. "You're not listening, old man."

"Quite the contrary. I heard everything clearly, but threats don't faze me. I've heard too many in my long life to care about one more."

With a disappointed shake of his head Luak dropped

the crystal on the floor, and it tinked and then clattered along the floor, rolling away until it hit the wall. Fyrn instinctively cringed at such a powerful object being so casually chucked aside, but it further proved his suspicion that Luak—thankfully—had no idea what he had in his possession.

The elf rolled up his sleeves, and dread shot clear to Fyrn's toes. His veins turned to ice when he saw the two Rhazdon Artifacts embedded in Luak's forearms. One spiraled up his arm like a golden snake, and the other looked like a golden talisman fused with his skin. Dark purple veins spiraled away from them as though they were filled with poison.

Fyrn couldn't help himself—he gaped. He'd suspected Luak had more than one Rhazdon Artifact, but neither of these were the legendary Firestarter—the one that gave him his fire magic. These were different.

That meant Luak had at least *three* Rhazdon Artifacts, which would make him almost impossible to defeat—even for Victoria.

"I've failed you," he said, too softly for even himself to hear.

And he had. Somehow, someway, he should have seen this coming and prepared Victoria appropriately.

He simply hadn't.

Luak's sneer widened. "You haven't seen what I'm capable of, old man. I will get the info I need, one way or another. How much pain that causes you is entirely up to you. Now, shall we begin?"

CHAPTER FIVE

Diesel pressed against a castle wall, ears twitching as they strained to hear through the enchanted peephole into one of the palace's war rooms.

He narrowed his eyes and peered into the room. To the dozen elves seated at the table, his peephole was nothing more than an eye in a painting on the wall. They wouldn't see him move or hear him breathe, but he would know everything that happened.

Being a confidant to the former king had had its privileges, and Diesel probably knew more about the castle than the deceased ruler himself.

He faltered, eyes dropping to the floor as he recalled seeing his friend's body on the ground in Lochrose. Truth be told, King Bornt had been a terrible monarch with little political expertise, and Diesel had told him as much when he was alive. They had been friends, and his friend was gone.

At least he'd had a proper burial with the witches and

wizards of Lochrose. He would be remembered, even if Diesel couldn't tell anyone he was dead.

Not yet.

Doing so would reveal his connection to Victoria and, more importantly, her newly-acquired Rhazdon Artifact. Those back at the safehouse might accept her, but most of Fairhaven would not.

The door on the far side opened, and Diesel tensed as Luak entered the room. Everyone stiffened in their seats, and even Diesel held his breath. He channeled his frustrated hatred into his hands, tightening them into fists in lieu of doing something stupid to the Light Elf who wanted to murder the love of his life.

Victoria may not have had any feelings for Diesel, but he would protect her regardless.

"We have two public enemies at large," Luak said, his eyes sweeping the faces at the table, "and as of now there has been no progress in finding them. How is it that two little girls have escaped Fairhaven's finest minds?"

Diesel nearly laughed. Luak had killed most of the brightest people in Fairhaven during his little coup—the one where Diesel had been on the hit list. If he hadn't been visiting Victoria when the murders took place, he very well might have died with the rest of them.

"We're searching, Lord Luak," a shrill voice said. Diesel tilted his head and saw a goblin he hadn't noticed before in the corner.

"Enough," an elf with broad shoulders said as he stood. It was Eldrin, one of the lieutenant generals of the army. His chair scraped the floor as he glowered at Luak. "You have spoken for the king far too often for my liking. We're waging a war against a hero of this town, and even if she is a Rhazdon host I will have no more of your lies! I *will* speak to the king!"

To his credit, Luak didn't flinch. He didn't so much as blink. He simply nodded ever so subtly toward the elf, who had rested his large hands on the table.

At the silent command, four ogres burst into the room and swarmed the elf too quickly for him to protest. Everyone else leaned away. Diesel craned his neck, but he could only see the hulking shoulders and dirt-stained armor of the ogres as they loomed over the dissenter.

When they parted, the elf lay unconscious on the ground. Two grabbed his arms and dragged him from the room, likely never to be seen again.

This charade wouldn't last. It wouldn't be long before Luak declared himself King of Fairhaven outright.

"Would anyone else like to speak to the king?" Luak asked kindly, eyebrows lifting as he scanned the room. "Come, now, don't be shy."

Every pair of eyes drifted to the floor, and Diesel fumed. Eldrin was a hero, an elf who had defended Fairhaven at every opportunity, and he didn't deserve this fate. Diesel would have to see if he could get him out of the dungeons.

He slunk down the hallway, doing his best to keep up with the ogres as they descended the stairs. The thin passage was barely wide enough for him to walk through, much less run, and he found himself sliding sideways along the narrower portions as he checked any peephole he could find to track their progress.

Finally they reached the dungeons, and they threw

Eldrin into the first available cell. Most were locked, their inmates huddled in the shadows. Diesel scanned the bars, wondering when he could slip in to—

"For the old wizard," a man said.

Diesel's heart skipped a beat as he froze. There was only one old wizard in Fairhaven.

He craned his neck to find the speaker—an elf who held a tray of moldy bread and black water. One of the ogres nodded him through, and he disappeared into the flickering shadows cast by the sparse fires in the sconces along the wall.

"Dinner's ready, Fyrn," the elf said with a sneer, his voice echoing down the hall.

Diesel's throat went dry and dread shot clear to his toes. He ran his hands through his hair, barely able to contain the rising panic in his chest.

They had Fyrn. He had to tell Victoria *immediately*.

CHAPTER SIX

Victoria paced the safehouse kitchen, biting her thumbnail nervously. Styx had gone to find the fairies and search for Fyrn, but Victoria could only retreat to the safehouse and try to come up with a plan. Bertha and Audrey sat at the dining table, but no one spoke.

After all, what was there to say? The general sense of panic and disbelief were almost too much to bear.

Luak had Fyrn. Their strongest ally. The most knowledgeable person not just about magic and war, but also about Fairhaven.

Her mentor.

"What are we going to do?" she asked the women at the table.

Audrey dropped her head into both hands, nervously drumming her fingers on her hairline as she stared at the grain of the wood. "You're the smart one, Victoria. If anyone can figure out how to proceed, it's you."

"Where is Diesel?" Bertha asked.

Victoria shrugged and spun on her heel to pace the

length of the kitchen again. "I haven't heard from him in about a day. He was going to infiltrate the castle and get us intel on the war room meetings."

Audrey slumped in her seat. "What if… What if Luak…"

"No, don't even start," Victoria said sharply. She glared at Audrey, unwilling to even entertain the possibility that Diesel had been captured as well.

Footsteps raced up the stairs from the basement, which held the entrance to the passage into the tunnels. All three women stood and braced themselves for whatever was about to round the corner.

Diesel flung himself through the doorway, hand on the frame to slow his approach as he slid along the floor. His chest heaved, and Victoria couldn't deny the wave of relief that crashed through her at seeing him safe and sound.

But they had business to attend to.

"Luak has Fyrn!" she and Diesel said at the same time.

Victoria hesitated. She was caught a little off-guard that he knew already, and he looked just as surprised that *she* did. The expression lasted only a moment, though, before it was replaced by his trademark grin.

"You're so clever," he said with a wink.

She set her hands on her hips. "This is serious. Focus."

His smile fell, and he nodded. "You're right, it's bad. If Luak was able to defeat Fyrn, it's only a matter of time before he comes for us all."

"We have to get him out of there," Victoria said, pacing some more.

"You're right again," Diesel said, "and I know who can help us."

Victoria quirked an eyebrow, not entirely sure she liked where this conversation was going. "Who?"

"The Speaker of the Senate, Lady Spry, is still alive. She's loyal to Fairhaven and whatever will preserve the liberties of the people. She will help us."

"Whoa, no way," Victoria said, lifting a hand to stop that train of thought in its tracks. "She's still breathing because Luak thinks she can be useful to him. He's not going to keep anyone alive who will stand against him."

Diesel grinned. "Lady Spry is one of the women he's trying to woo. He wants her as his queen—or maybe one of many. He fancies her, and underestimates her cunning. That's why she's still alive."

Victoria laughed. "Luak doesn't strike me as the romantic type, Diesel."

"It's true," Bertha piped up. "Lady Spry has had hundreds of suitors over the years. There are rumors that she can enrapture any man. She's a clever woman, and if Diesel trusts her, so do I."

Victoria crossed her arms and bit her lip as she processed this new idea. She didn't like trusting new people, much less someone in Luak's inner circle. This was too much, too fast.

But if they wanted to save Fyrn, they didn't have the luxury of time. They had to act quickly, before…

She swallowed hard to suppress the thought of losing him to a monster like Luak, and called upon the gifts in her bear figurine to think clearly and calmly. She had to make a logical choice, not an emotional one.

As her nerves simmered, she closed her eyes and reviewed what she knew.

Fyrn was locked in the dungeons.

Diesel could get them inside.

Lady Spry had contacts on the inside and could pull strings to get Fyrn out safely—probably.

"What would Lady Spry do for us?" Victoria asked.

"Distract Luak," Diesel said. "He'll be expecting a rescue attempt. He'll be expecting *you*. I think this is a trap, Victoria, and we need all the help we can get to keep him away from you."

Victoria nodded. It made sense. With her panic and fear at bay, she could finally see this for what it was: a crazy-as-fuck plan, but the only one they had.

And it all came down to this new woman—Lady Spry, a politician Victoria had never met.

"Get her," Victoria ordered, "and bring her here. I want to talk to her myself."

Audrey scribbled down some ideas on how to get Fyrn out of the castle dungeon, but so far her notes looked more like doodles of explosions and an angry stick figure of Luak dressed as the Queen of Hearts, shouting, "Off with her head!"

It wasn't as cathartic as Audrey had envisioned it would be.

Victoria sat at the head of the table fuming, arms crossed as she stared at a charred plate of...well, *something* in front of her. Audrey wasn't quite sure what it was, but it looked like it had once been oatmeal. Behind her, Bertha whisked a bowl of something sugary. Plumes of white powder flew into the air as she stared absently at the wall.

No one here handled stress well.

The door to the basement creaked open, and everyone stood. Chairs scraped the floor as swords were drawn, or in Victoria's case, summoned. Audrey held her breath as they waited for whoever had joined them to show their face.

A regal woman stepped into the kitchen, her back erect as she surveyed the room. Her dark eyes rested momentarily on Audrey's face and then flitted to the tiara on her head, but Audrey wasn't about to hide what she was. Not here.

This was *her* territory.

The woman's white robes had gold hems that slid along the ground as she stepped into the kitchen. Her dark hair had been pinned into a bun, which showed off her slender neck as she took a soft breath and bowed her head.

"Ladies," she said, her voice like honey.

Damn. Soft, elegant, graceful…no wonder this classy chick had all the men. Audrey sheathed her sword and crossed her arms, trying to rein in a sudden wave of envy she didn't fully understand.

Diesel appeared behind her, all smiles. "See, I told you she would help us!"

Victoria walked toward the woman with her shoulders squared and a glare on her face that could melt snow. "And how do we know you won't go to Luak when you're done here?"

Diesel's smile fell. "Victoria, please…"

"No, it's all right," Lady Spry said with a gentle nod of

her head. "You are wise to be worried, Victoria, but I assure you I want that Light Elf dead. However I can prove myself to you, I will."

Victoria nodded and said without breaking eye contact, "Diesel, make a favor pact between the lady and me."

"What?" Diesel's jaw dropped open. "Do you understand who this—"

"I know who she is, Diesel, and as insurance she is going to owe me a favor—one I will return to her when Fyrn is safely home."

A thin, almost relieved smile spread across the woman's face, and Audrey couldn't help but be impressed. Nothing fazed this woman.

"Gladly," Lady Spry said. "I understand your caution, Victoria, and I will happily do this for you if it means we both get what we want."

"And what do *you* want?" Victoria asked, standing a bit taller.

"Luak dead. Fairhaven returned to its former peaceful state. A new monarch on the throne."

Audrey's shoulders drooped, as did Diesel's. Poor King Bornt.

"I have a better idea," Diesel said, eyes glazing over momentarily as he lost himself to thought. "A binding agreement."

Victoria finally broke eye contact with the Speaker of the Senate to stare at him blankly. "A what?"

"A magical legal agreement that binds us to its terms," Lady Spry said. "I would accept this."

Victoria crossed her arms, apparently not satisfied yet. "What happens if you break the agreement?"

"Instant death."

Audrey rolled her eyes. "Only in Fairhaven."

Hands on her hips, Victoria lifted her chin defiantly. "Fine. My terms are this: you never speak of anything we discuss to anyone unless I, Diesel, or Audrey are present. You will see to it that Fyrn is freed, regardless of the cost to you."

The noblewoman nodded. "And my terms are this: you will depose Luak and see to it he is killed for his crimes against Fairhaven, even if you must deliver the final blow yourself. You will do everything in your power to find a worthwhile successor and protect Fairhaven and its people until your dying day."

Victoria's shoulders relaxed ever so slightly and her expression softened. Not in horror, as Audrey's would have, but in relief. "That's what you want?"

Lady Spry smiled. "It is all I have ever wanted. You and I will find a suitable replacement for the late King Bornt, and you will continue to protect Fairhaven even after the replacement is found."

Victoria smiled. "I think we have a deal."

The woman offered her hand, and Victoria shook it. As their skin touched, their eyes glowed white. Runes appeared on their arms and trailed up their necks, and Victoria froze in place. Lady Spry simply closed her eyes, as if this were routine and perhaps a bit enjoyable.

Audrey stiffened, but Diesel gently shook his head. "It's fine," he mouthed.

Not entirely convinced, Audrey kept one hand on the hilt of her sword, ready to strike at a moment's notice.

Within seconds, the glow began to fade. Victoria

relaxed, and Lady Spry swayed slightly. Diesel set his hand on her shoulder to steady her, and she flashed him a grateful smile before returning her attention to Victoria.

"It appears we have a deal," Lady Spry said.

"It seems so," Victoria said, leaning on the table for balance. She looked about ready to go to sleep, but powered through. If it had winded Victoria even with the bear figurine's magic, that must have been a powerful spell.

"Diesel informed me of the plan on the way here," Lady Spry said, apparently all business. "I will distract Luak as best I can, delaying him until the last possible minute. When I have an opportunity to do so, I will send word to you by my pixie, Lori."

A small head appeared from the folds of Lady Spry's robes and the pixie nervously peeked around the fabric as if she didn't want to emerge. Her long red hair flowed around her shoulders and her wings buzzed to life, lifting her into the air near her master's face. The little pixie wore a knee-length green gown and waved sheepishly to the crowd of giants around her.

From his place on the table, Styx's jaw dropped. He ran a hand through his hair, and seconds later a dumb smile appeared on his face.

Apparently the little guy was smitten. Audrey chuckled.

"When Lori comes to you, you must act quickly and get in as fast as possible."

"We should station ourselves by the castle, then," Victoria said, tapping her finger on her lips. "When will you be able to distract him?"

"As early as tonight, and tomorrow at the latest."

Victoria nodded and spun on her heel. "Get ready,

everyone. We're going to go rescue that old fart. We'll meet back here in twenty."

Bertha stood, and Victoria bounded up the stairs—that glazed look in her eyes evidence that she was already lost in thought and coming up with various plans of attack should things fall through.

Diesel gestured for the Speaker of the Senate to descend the stairs to the basement again, but Audrey set one hand on the woman's shoulder before she could leave. The noblewoman lifted one delicate eyebrow in curiosity.

"Thank you," Audrey said simply.

Lady Spry smiled and nodded wordlessly.

With that, Audrey left them to their devices. Diesel had to get the woman back to the castle, and Audrey had to prepare for war.

***

Regina Spry reclined on one of the luxurious couches in her chambers and stared out the window at her home city. She had lived here her entire life, one of the only witches afforded the honor of ascending to Fairhaven's nobility.

In her childhood years, Fairhaven had been a loud place full of shops and the clinking tinkle of denni changing hands. There had been laughter, and as a little girl she had run through the streets with her elfin friends every weekend on the way to the sweets shops.

But now her beautiful city lay in ruins. Boards covered most windows, and she hadn't seen an open store in over a week. Luak just stole what he needed, so most commerce had stopped completely. He was starving the people to weaken their resolve while he took over every inch of the city.

Not if she could help it.

Regina had played Luak's game. She had feigned flattery at his advances, blaming her traditional upbringing for her aloofness and need to take any relationship slowly. And it had worked—until now. Luak would soon grow impatient and Regina would have to choose: Fairhaven or Luak.

She would always choose Fairhaven, even if it meant her death.

Someone knocked on her door, and she snapped her fingers to open it. No door could be locked any more—at least not in the castle—and she knew better than to try to deny entry to any of Luak's guards. Every time someone knocked on her door, she could only pray it wasn't Luak.

Thankfully, a stranger stood at her door—an elf dressed in the black armor of the palace mercenaries.

She stood, waiting for him to speak.

"All council members are to report to the throne room, Lady Spry," the elf said with a gesture toward the hallway.

She nodded and obeyed wordlessly, allowing him to walk ahead of her. It took everything in her power not to panic, but this was it—the final overt show of power. No one had been in the throne room since King Bornt disappeared, since the only reason to go would be to speak with the king.

Or in this case, the new king.

Luak would declare himself ruler of Fairhaven, the final blow to the city's freedom.

As the mercenary walked ahead of her, Regina tapped her sleeve. Lori slid out of the robe and flew off in the opposite direction, keeping close to the ceiling to avoid detection.

There would be no better moment than this to rescue Fyrn. Luak would be decently distracted, and she would congratulate him afterward to ensure he remained unaware of the rescue attempt beneath his nose for as long as possible.

A wave of nausea burned in her throat at the thought of congratulating the murderer on his ascension to the throne, but she calmly reminded herself of the game. She would play Luak for everything he was worth, and then she would replace him with someone far superior.

Victoria.

If anyone could save Fairhaven and return it to greatness, it was the Rhazdon host who had won the hearts of so many citizens. They loved her, and Victoria had just sworn to protect the city on pain of death—a promise she had made without batting an eye, Regina had noted quite happily.

Yes, Victoria was perfect. She wouldn't want the job, of course, but that was what would make her the perfect queen.

CHAPTER SEVEN

Luak waited in a wing of the throne room as noblemen filled the space. There weren't enough to fill the room entirely, but he would bring in soldiers to fill the rest.

After all, he needed a full house for his coronation.

He grinned and ran his finger over the gold crown resting on a purple pillow on a nearby windowsill. The glittering light from the crystal overhead illuminated its brilliance, and the rubies glimmered as if full of fire.

How appropriate.

As the murmur in the hall faded, he straightened his back and walked into the throne room as though he owned it—because now, technically, he did.

The ornate golden throne sat in the middle of a raised platform, facing the hundreds of chairs that had been placed in the hall for his coronation. He loved that none of them knew what was about to happen, and he got to watch the slow march of horror across each face when the realization set in.

Luak sank into the thick red cushion on the throne's seat and placed his hands on the armrests. Chin lifted, he let his gaze linger on every face in the hall, relishing the blended expressions of terror and acceptance.

When he reached Lady Spry, however, he couldn't quite read her face. The expression seemed to be one of mild pride, and he nodded once to her. Her smile widened at his attention. Once this whole war business was over and Victoria's Rhazdon Artifact was his, he would finally have the time to enjoy himself—and his new kingdom's citizens—fully.

He could hardly wait.

One of his mercenaries carried the pillow with the crown from the wings and stopped before Luak, kneeling as he offered it. The gold shone even more brightly in the light radiating through the domed glass ceiling above, and Luak couldn't help himself.

As he placed the crown on his head, he sneered.

"There is a new law in Fairhaven," he said, voice booming in the magnificent throne room. "Mine."

"Bow before your king!" the mercenary ordered.

To Luak's delight, the surviving senators and noblemen slowly obeyed. One by one, they bowed before him.

Luak could taste victory. Once the girl was dead, nothing would stand in his way.

Victoria pressed her back against the wall, craning her neck to share a peephole with Diesel as they surveyed the dungeons.

The little pixie Lori had arrived mere moments ago while she, Audrey, and Diesel had paced the tunnel that would take them to the dungeons. Victoria flexed her fingers, itching for a fight. They had no time to spare.

"I've got the three on the left," Diesel said with a nod to the ogres along that wall.

"Then I'll take those," Victoria said with a nod to the four elves and two ogres along the opposite wall.

"Showoff," Diesel said with a grin.

She smirked.

"What about me?" Audrey asked, one foot propped against the wall as she leaned against it.

"Take out anyone who surprises us," Victoria suggested.

"Think there will be a lot of surprises?"

Diesel shrugged. "According to Lady Spry's intel Fyrn is in the high-risk cells, and those are difficult to break into. I'll be able to take down the charms, but it will take time before we can open the cell. You'll need to stave off any attacks and, by some miracle, get us back in here."

"There's no closer secret passage?" Victoria asked.

"Afraid not, my love," Diesel said.

Victoria rolled her eyes. "Will you give it up?"

"Guys, come on," Audrey said with a gesture toward the peephole.

Victoria sighed. "Ready?"

"As I'll ever be," Audrey said with a shrug.

Victoria laughed. "That's the spirit."

With a snap of Diesel's fingers, the secret door slid open. As stone grated against stone, Victoria leapt into the dungeon and summoned her sword. A hail of white and blue spells flew around her, and in seconds the dungeon had become a war zone.

Bodies fell. Men groaned in pain. Swords clashed. Victoria ducked every blow that came her way, and each sword was a second too late when the mercenaries tried to gut her. One ogre charged her, and for fun she merely held her ground. He hit her as though she were a brick wall and crumpled at her feet, no match for the strength in her bear figurine.

Her allotted six guards taken care of, Victoria charged in the direction Diesel had suspected Fyrn's cell lay while Audrey and Diesel handled the remaining soldiers. A few more funneled in from the hallway to see what the commotion was about, but none of them made it back out.

In the rearmost cells there was no light except for the thin beams of daylight that filtered through the narrow window at the top of each cell. It was hardly enough to see by, so Victoria found herself squinting into the shadows of every cell in the hunt for her mentor. The longer she walked, the less she heard the commotion from the front of the dungeons. Back here, there was little noise besides a steady drip of water somewhere in the depths and the occasional cough of a prisoner.

"Fyrn!" she hissed, panic again rising in her chest.

She passed several more cells, and only a few strangers approached the bars. No one spoke, and they watched her with wary eyes. It seemed as though they wondered if this was a trick, something Luak had planned to test their loyalties. Covered in dirt, they kept mostly to the shadows, and she couldn't make out any faces.

"Fyrn! Damn it, where are you?" she asked the darkness.

"Victoria?" an old man's voice replied.

"Fyrn!" She hurried toward the voice and found a heap of clothes lying on the stone floor, chest just barely moving with a steady rhythm. It took her a moment to realize it was a body covered in rags, too weak to move.

"Fyrn!"

"Victoria, you must…you must run, child. Run!" he said weakly.

Fuck. That.

Victoria grabbed the bars with her hands. Jolts of electricity burned through her, but she gritted through the pain and allowed her first Rhazdon Artifact to heal her even as the magic cooked her skin. It was painful, but she wouldn't die.

Using all the strength she could muster from the bear figurine, she pulled on the metal door. The hinges groaned, the lock splintered, the bars began to bend, and the entire door slowly yielded to her newfound strength.

With a final heave, she wrenched the door from its hinges.

As it clattered to the floor, Victoria ran into the room and lifted Fyrn's shoulders. The old wizard didn't protest, and as she examined his face in the low light he seemed three hundred years older. He had more wrinkles, and he couldn't even lift his head.

"What did Luak do to you?" she whispered, horrified.

"Run. Run," he muttered, eyes drifting closed.

Okay, they would talk later then.

Victoria lifted him, and with her enhanced strength it was as though he weighed nothing. She held him closely and ran through the hall, back to the secret passageway and the chaos waiting for her there.

As she rounded the final corner, all hell broke loose.

"Victoria, go!" Diesel shouted. He had taken cover by the stairs and was hiding behind a wall as a volley of spells were shot at him. During every break in the attack he lobbed a massive ball of white energy at them, and screams followed.

Audrey jumped into the passageway as Victoria neared, gesturing wildly for her to follow. "Come on! Come on, Victoria, *move!*"

Victoria leapt in just as an explosion knocked Diesel onto his back. He slid along the ground and hit his head against the wall, cursing to himself as he nursed the ache.

"Diesel, come on!" she shouted.

"Go! Take Eldrin and go!"

She frowned. "Who the fuck is Eldrin?"

"That guy," Audrey said, nodding to an unconscious elf slumped farther down the tunnel.

Another explosion rocked the dungeon, and Diesel caught Victoria's eye. With a snap of his fingers, the door shut in her face, sealing her in the secret tunnel.

"No!" she screamed, jamming her shoulder against the sealed passage.

The wall shook, but Audrey stepped between her and the door before she could ram it again. "Victoria, he can get out, okay? We discussed this when things went south. You and I need to get out of here, and I can't carry this Eldrin dude, all right? I need you. Focus! Diesel will get out!"

Victoria gritted her teeth. As shouts carried through the door, she adjusted her grip on Fyrn so she could throw

Eldrin over her shoulder. They ran down the hall to the tunnels, Victoria swearing that she would rip the castle apart if they imprisoned Diesel, too.

Victoria sat in one of the kitchen chairs, biting her lip and bouncing her knee as she stared at the basement door, waiting for Diesel to burst through.

"We have to go back," she said.

Audrey leaned against the wall, her body as tense as Victoria felt. After a moment of silence, the Atlantean girl nodded. "Yeah, I think so. I'll go get my—"

The door was flung open and Diesel fell on the floor, chest heaving and blood dripping from his nose. He looked as though he had run a marathon, and clutched his side as Victoria rushed to him. "Diesel!"

He grinned through the pain and winked at her. "Were you worried about me, my love? I knew you cared."

She ignored him and lifted his shirt to see the wound beneath his hand.

He laughed. "So frisky, my darling? Can't wait to welcome me home?"

"Oh, for the love of God, shut up and let us heal you," Victoria snapped, slapping away his hand so she could see the wound.

He shook his head. "I can heal myself. I merely need a moment."

"Don't be stubborn. We'll—"

"Victoria," he said gently.

She hesitated, catching his gaze. He watched her calmly,

and it settled her nerves. He smiled. "I will heal myself, thank you."

Her shoulders relaxed, and she nodded. "I think Fyrn needs you too. Bertha's doing her best, but your magic would be helpful."

Diesel nodded and stood, leaning on Victoria as she guided him toward Fyrn's makeshift hospital bed in the back bedroom. She suspected Diesel didn't need to lean on her, but she couldn't deny how grateful she was that the asshole was okay.

When they entered Fyrn's room, Bertha sighed with relief and stepped back. "Diesel, help him."

Fyrn laid in the bed with the covers up to his chest, the filthy rags replaced with a clean shirt. The lines in his face cast deep shadows, and his chest rose gently as he slumbered.

Diesel limped toward the old wizard and set one hand on the man's chest. The crystal in the tip of his staff glowed, and a gentle hum filled the room.

Fyrn gasped violently, and his eyes shot open. He tried to sit up, but groaned in pain and fell back against the pillow.

"Hush, hush. Be still," Bertha chided.

"Fyrn!" Victoria said, a relieved smile breaking across her face.

Fyrn's shoulders rose and fell with his exaggerated breaths, and it hurt Victoria to watch him struggle.

"What did Luak do to you?" she asked.

"He's a monster," Fyrn said softly. "He's far more powerful than I realized."

"Awesome," Audrey said from the doorway, pinching the bridge of her nose in frustration.

Victoria's jaw tensed, but they had to find out what Fyrn knew. "What do you mean? Has he acquired more soldiers?"

Fyrn shook his head, unable to keep his eyes open as he spoke. "He has four Rhazdon Artifacts, Victoria. *Four*. He's a master of fire, water, torture, and metal. Your two are not enough to destroy him."

Bertha gasped, and Victoria's hands balled into fists. After everything she had endured, after all the sacrifice…

She wasn't enough.

Victoria gritted her teeth. "What do I have to do?"

"There isn't time," Fyrn said with a weak gesture toward the wall, though he had no doubt meant to gesture toward the castle. "We must attack. We must… We must…"

Fyrn's breathing settled into a slow and steady pace and Victoria watched her mentor as he slept, utterly destroyed by whatever Luak had done. It seemed as though Fyrn wasn't long for this world, but Victoria would do everything in her power to save him.

CHAPTER EIGHT

Victoria couldn't take it anymore. She had to check on Fyrn.

The door to his room had been closed for hours, and only Bertha or Diesel had been allowed in to check on him. Victoria had tried to train, to cook, to do anything besides worry—and while her bear figurine's magic helped keep the nerves from overwhelming her entirely, a low level of anxiety still hummed like a fly in her ear.

The door creaked as she entered, and she pulled the chair in the corner over to his bedside. At first he continued to snooze, arms resting peacefully on his stomach as his chest rose and fell, but after a while his eyes fluttered open.

"Victoria?"

"Hey," she said softly. She tried to smile, but it came out as more of a nervous twitch.

"You look terrible," he wheezed with a laugh.

She chuckled. "Can't really sleep when I have you to worry about, can I?"

He weakly waved away her concern, though he was not strong enough to lift his hand more than a few inches. "I'm fine."

"Hardly. You look like you had the life sucked out of you."

Fyrn sighed and tilted his head slightly. "Something like that."

"What did he do to you?"

"What's missing, Victoria? What do I not have on me now that I've had with me every time we've ever spoken?"

She scanned his face, confused by the question. "You don't have anything on you. Your hat, your robe, your staff—"

"Exactly," he said.

"What, your staff?"

Fyrn nodded. "Victoria, what I am about to tell you is an absolute secret. You can tell no one, not even Diesel. Not even Audrey. Do you understand?"

"But—"

"Please, Victoria," he said with a cough. His eyes fluttered closed. "Please."

She sighed, shoulders hunched in defeat. "Fine, Fyrn. It's our secret."

"Good, good," he said softly. "My staff was no ordinary weapon. Witches and wizards can use staffs in lieu of wands, yes, but mine was special."

"What do you mean?"

A mischievous smile tugged at the corners of Fyrn's mouth, twitching as it fought to spread across his tired features. "My staff was a powerful artifact fused with an even more powerful relic. Do you remember what those are?"

"I think so," she said, a little hesitant. "An artifact is like a flashlight, and the relic is the battery, right?"

Fyrn nodded. "Just like your Rhazdon Artifact, child. You are the battery."

She shuddered involuntarily, not entirely liking that fact.

"My staff," Fyrn continued, "housed one of the most powerful relics known. Paired with the right artifact, it could decimate entire cities. It has immense power, Victoria, and it has kept me alive all these years."

Victoria scanned his weathered face as she tried to process what he had said. "It keeps you alive?"

He nodded. "I'm far older than I seem, Victoria. By any reasonable expectation, I should not have lived this long. That relic, and that alone, has kept me alive, and if I do not get it back I won't live long enough to see you depose Luak."

Victoria stared at him in stunned silence as she processed this news. "But...but..."

Fyrn lifted a weak hand, his fingers shaking as they reached for her. She took it, careful to hold him gently and not crush his hand with her enhanced strength.

"I'm so impressed with you," he said, smiling. "I believe in you. I believe in your strength. In your kindness. In your courage. You are a brave soul, my dear, and you will never fail those you love, not even if you try. You're a good soul— a strong soul—and it has been an honor to teach you."

Weakened and at death's door, his grumpy personality

had all but faded. He had things to say, and he didn't know if he would have another chance to say them.

She swallowed hard. "Those sound like final words."

His eyes shut. "I hope they aren't, my girl, but I had to say them just in case."

In the silence, Victoria held his hand. He slowly relaxed and his breathing evened out, and he once more fell asleep. Tenderly, Victoria returned his hand to his stomach and squared her shoulders.

"I won't let you down, Fyrn," she swore. "I won't let you die."

Diesel led the way as he and Victoria ran down one of the castle's secret passages toward one of the castle's many treasure vaults. She had asked Audrey and Styx to stay behind to protect Fyrn and the safehouse, a request that had involved a shouting match and a few glares.

But they had to face the facts: Diesel knew the castle and Audrey didn't. Audrey could take out a city block with her magic, and the safehouse needed guarding. And Styx… Well, he could distract Audrey from her fuming.

Besides, even Diesel didn't know what they were looking for, not really. He thought they were merely searching for Fyrn's staff, since a wizard's magical instrument was a source of pride, something he didn't easily part with.

Only Victoria knew better.

"You know," Diesel said between huffs of breath as they

ran, "you don't need to go on life or death missions to spend time with me."

She rolled her eyes.

"Seriously," he continued. "I have twenty-seven better date ideas. Some of them even involve me cooking food for you. Me! Cooking! For you!"

"Focus," she chided.

"As you desire, my darling," he said, slowing to take one of the side passages off the secret hallway.

She followed, not sure if it was worth looking in any more of the vaults. There were seventeen in total, according to Diesel, but there was no guarantee he knew of them all.

In the back of her mind, a flicker of inspiration hovered just out of reach. The familiar feeling burned within her, nostalgic and almost painful. She gasped, slowing and holding her head as she struggled to understand it.

As she sat with the feeling, it melted through her like ice on a hot sidewalk. It was an incredible sensation that became a robust sense of knowing, an unspoken understanding of something great.

"Gah," she muttered to herself, fighting through the odd sensation.

"What is it?" Diesel set a hand on each of her shoulders, but she closed her eyes to focus on it.

Her intuition flared. This was important. She needed to push through this.

The flicker of inspiration neared, as though someone were handing her the answer on a silver platter...if only she could reach it.

Her eyes shot open as clarity crashed through her. "I know where Fyrn's staff is."

"What? How could you possibly—"

"Luak's room. Do you know where that is?"

Victoria was grinning with excitement. The moment of clarity had been so invigorating, so overpowering that she could barely contain herself. It only made sense—defeating someone as powerful as Fyrn was quite an accomplishment, one Luak would brag about for the rest of his life. The staff—the symbol of the wizard's power that would outlive even him—was a trophy.

One he would keep close to him as a daily reminder of his greatness.

Diesel stuttered. "*Luak's* room? Why on Earth—"

"It's there. I know it is."

Diesel gaped at her for a moment before gathering himself enough to snap his mouth shut. "Yes, I can take you there."

The confirmation sent a humming vibration deep into her core, and the bear figurine buzzed with excitement. It was confirmation that this hunch of hers was solid.

The relic would be there.

Diesel could not believe he was about to break into the king's chambers. Sure, he knew *how,* but knowledge was entirely separate from action.

The things he did for this woman.

Victoria peeked out of the secret passage. "Coast is clear."

"Victoria, please rethink this. He will know the moment we enter that room."

"I figured."

"We can't stay. If the staff isn't immediately visible, we may have to leave without it. The charms guarding the door are silent and powerful, and nothing I can do will keep them from going off."

She looked at him, all serious beauty. "Diesel, we'll be fine. Remember, the staff was destroyed. We just need to get his crystal thingy."

At that Diesel couldn't help but smile. She was human, after all—she didn't know about the magic of staffs or wizards, not really. "Get crystal thingy. Don't die. Got it."

"Har har. Now come on, move!"

Diesel kicked in Luak's door, and a burst of magic cut through him. It was like a punch to the gut, but Victoria didn't seem to feel it. Unsurprising, as wizard's magic was usually undetectable to non-wizards, but it still knocked the wind out of him. He lost several valuable seconds as he caught his breath.

Victoria had already overturned three sofas and a table by the time Diesel joined her. He ripped through the sitting room, using every spell he could think of to magically shred cushions and open drawers, but he kept most of his attention on the hallway and the still-open secret passage as the moments passed.

They didn't have long.

"Found it!" Victoria shouted from the other room.

"Victoria, not so loud!" Diesel hissed.

She ran around the corner with the familiar crystal in her hands, and lifted it for Diesel to examine. He nodded.

"Definitely it, now let's go."

Her gaze shifted to the hallway, and he could almost read her thoughts. She wanted to stay. To fight.

"Another day, Victoria," he said softly.

She tensed her jaw and nodded, running ahead of him into the passage. He slid in and snapped his fingers, commanding the door to shut with a silent spell. As it soundlessly closed, he let out a breath of relief.

They had managed to be in and out in mere minutes, a truly phenomenal feat.

"Now, let's get—"

Diesel was interrupted by the thump of feet in the corridor, and peeked through an enchanted spyhole at the army racing down the hallway with Luak in the lead. He stormed into the decimated bedroom, fuming.

"Find whoever did this and drag them by the throat to me!" he screamed.

Diesel turned his gaze on Victoria, who shared the spyhole with him. Her body had gone rigid, and Diesel wondered if she would plow through the wall. After all, this was the elf who had not only threatened her life many times, but who had murdered her parents in front of her. Victoria had a vendetta, a bloodlust she needed to satisfy, and only killing Luak would give her that peace.

Diesel set his hand on her shoulder, and she flinched as her eyes met his. He could guess exactly what she was thinking—*I want his head on a platter.*

"You're not ready," Diesel said softly.

She frowned, glaring at him with an icy expression that nearly frosted his skin. After a few tense moments, however, she nodded. "I know. Fyrn said Luak has immense power, and I need to get stronger first. I'm not going to take on a monster I'm not ready to slay."

Diesel let out a long sigh of relief. "Let's get the old fart his crystal thingy, huh?"

Victoria chuckled, and she took the lead as they jogged back the way they had come. Diesel loved how comfortable she was when she was in charge—even if she *was* going the wrong way.

CHAPTER NINE

Audrey reclined in one of the kitchen chairs, one eyebrow lifted in disbelief as she stared at Lady Spry. "There are others?"

The regal woman nodded. "Many fled to the tunnels as Luak's mercenaries took over the city, and they need to be united. They live in isolated pockets of—"

The door to the basement swung open, and Victoria raced through with Diesel hot on her heels. Though she breathed normally Diesel huffed, hands on his knees as he fought to catch his breath.

"Luak is pissed," Victoria said with a grin, lifting the crystal that had once sat atop Fyrn's staff.

"I'm going to take a nap," Diesel said, wheezing. He headed for the living room, only to stop when he scanned the table.

Audrey grinned, watching Lady Spry, Bertha, and Edgar from her peripheral vision. They had all taken seats when the senator had unexpectedly arrived with surprising news.

"What's going on?" Diesel asked.

"Apparently there are more in hiding, like us," Audrey said, tilting her head toward the senator.

Lady Spry nodded. "I recently uncovered what I suspect are the secret rebel hideouts of those who couldn't find a way to leave the city but didn't want to live under Luak's rule. They've escaped to many of the deepest, most difficult-to-reach caverns beneath the city. They can help you —and I believe you can help them."

Victoria stood a little taller as the senator looked directly at her.

"How did you find them?" Bertha asked.

The lady's shoulders drooped. "I uncovered new information about the hunt for Victoria and Audrey. Luak is furious at Fyrn's rescue, and he intends to go through every house in the city, starting with the deserted ones. He's coming here, so you absolutely must leave. I needed to find you someplace else to go, and though these are only suspicions, I believe I am correct in assuming there are rebels in these caverns who can hide you."

"Damn it," Victoria muttered. She rubbed her temples, still cradling the crystal in one hand.

"We should leave," Bertha said softly.

Audrey nodded. "The sooner the better."

"Everyone, pack," Victoria said. "We won't have to run for much longer."

Audrey perked up, leaning her elbows on the table as she leaned toward her friend. "What do you mean?"

"I've had a few ideas," Victoria said with a smirk. "Go get ready. I'll update you in a minute, once I get this crystal to Fyrn."

"Reginald and Greggor are still in the tunnels," Edgar said with a nod toward the basement. "I will wait for them as long as I can and meet up with you."

"Very good," Lady Spry said, standing.

Audrey watched Victoria as she headed for Fyrn's bedroom. She was so confident, so focused. So ready for battle. It made Audrey proud to see Victoria so effortlessly taking command.

With her in charge, they would be fine.

Victoria gently shut the door behind her as she tiptoed into Fyrn's room. He slept in the bed, and she wanted to prolong whatever rest he could get.

"How did it go?" Fyrn asked, eyes still closed.

Victoria chuckled and set the crystal on his lap. "Just fine."

He sighed with relief, apparently too tired to open his eyes, but his hands found the relic and held it tightly. "Thank you, Victoria. Thank you."

"Diesel helped."

Fyrn laughed. "I'm too proud to thank him. He knows."

Victoria rolled her eyes, but her smile didn't linger. "We're moving you, since apparently Luak is getting more violent in his hunt for us."

"Unsurprising."

"We're going to the tunnels. Possibly there are rebels there who can help us."

"Good, good," Fyrn said softly.

"I'm going to have to carry you, aren't I?"

"Hell yes, you are," he muttered.

Victoria chuckled. "Fine, you big baby."

Fyrn smiled. "I suppose you're right. After all, I was merely tortured. No big deal."

"Totally," Victoria said with a sarcastic shrug.

The old wizard finally opened his eyes, and he inspected the relic in his hands. "Good, it's all here. Nothing broke."

"Would it still work if it had?"

"Yes, but not as well. This relic can never, ever be allowed to break," he said with a somber glance her way.

"Noted. What artifact are you going to fuse it with, do you know?"

Fyrn sighed. "I have a secret vault in the tunnels where I house my more powerful artifacts. Though I enjoyed and protected my home, I always knew it might be compromised. One of the hazards of being powerful is having many enemies. Though they likely stole everything, Luak found nothing useful there."

"Good," Victoria said, crossing her arms.

"I need you to take me to my artifact room, and then we will be done with this once and for all," Fyrn said, tapping the crystal.

"Of course," Victoria said. "Anything you need, Fyrn."

He smiled. "I knew I could count on you."

"So are we bonding, or are you going to be a grumpy asshole again once you have your staff?"

"Grumpy asshole," he said, settling into his pillow.

Victoria chuckled. Oh, good. She was worried his brush with death had made him all sappy and *nice.*

CHAPTER TEN

Victoria could hardly believe her eyes.

She stood at the entrance to a magnificent cave with a marvelous crystal in its ceiling. Though this one was a fraction of the size of Fairhaven's primary crystal, it glowed more intensely and lit the room with the fire of a star.

Fyrn's secret cavern—one of many, as Victoria was starting to discover—held incredible treasures. Several chests filled with gold and jewels sat in one corner. Weapons of every kind had been hung on the walls, and a walkway cut through the various piles of staffs, mirrors, and even stacks of furniture.

Victoria had bought a bit of time by asking everyone to wait for her and Fyrn to run a quick errand, but she'd had no idea they were headed someplace as grand as this.

From her shoulder, Styx gaped in awe. He squeaked, then jabbered as though she could understand him.

"What on earth…" Victoria lost her train of thought as she stared into the massive room.

From his place against the wall by the entrance, Fyrn shrugged. "You collect a lot of shit over the centuries. I had to put it somewhere."

"How rich *are* you?" Victoria raised one curious eyebrow at her mentor. To have bought all of this, he had to have had the wealth of a king.

"Very. Go," he said, with a nod to the piles.

"Where do I start?"

"I need another staff, and there are several over on the far wall. Pick a white one, if you please."

Victoria chuckled and obeyed, selecting a particularly elegant staff from among the ten that lay against the wall. Two were black, three were brown, and the final five were all white and had various runes etched into their bases. All had an opening at the top wide enough for the relic.

But this one—the elegant one—had a graceful tilt that reminded her of the elves. The end of the staff had tiny twirling ribbons of wood that almost looked like a cage, and the runes along its base glowed a vibrant blue even without anything powering it.

She offered the staff to her mentor, who nodded in approval. "Good choice, now stand back."

He lifted the relic in one hand and the staff in the other and began to mutter to himself in a language Victoria didn't recognize. Both objects began to glow brilliantly blue and Victoria squinted, the light too much to bear. Just then a blast of light cut through the entire room.

As it faded, Victoria slowly opened her eyes to find her mentor standing in front of her. He leaned on his staff as his body absorbed the light. His wrinkles faded, and the dark circles beneath his eyes brightened. The bruises from the torture had healed entirely, and he sucked in a deep breath as he stood upright.

"You're back!" Victoria said, a swell of joy overtaking her.

Fyrn nodded. "And I have you to thank, Victoria, but we will never speak of this again to anyone. No one can know what this relic is."

Victoria's smile faded, but she nodded. "I understand."

"Now, shall we go meet those rebels?" Fyrn asked, gesturing to the exit.

"Yes, let's," Victoria said with a grin.

At first Victoria thought they had gotten lost.

"There's nothing here," Audrey said, echoing Victoria's thoughts.

"There is," Lady Spry said with confidence, never once slowing in her steady march through the tunnels.

The tunnel was as dark as night, with only the glowing tips of the wizards' staffs to light the way. As they followed the noblewoman she withdrew a wand and flicked it, igniting the tip with a brilliant white glow that lit into the endless tunnel. Styx's wings beat the air nearby, but in the sparse light she couldn't even see him.

Everyone from the safehouse was behind Lady Spry, and Victoria couldn't help but be nervous. They were following someone they didn't know well—and who Victoria still didn't fully trust—into the recesses of the dangerous Fairhaven tunnels.

She almost stopped them right there. She almost called

this off, convinced she could find another safehouse, but she remembered the pact she and Lady Spry had made.

To betray them meant death for the noblewoman, and Victoria doubted Lady Spry cared enough for Luak to sacrifice herself.

Cautiously optimistic, Victoria glanced around. "Where are they? The rebels?"

Without answering, Lady Spry ran her hand along one of the walls, humming to herself as she fiddled with the protruding rocks. After a few moments of hunting, she finally pressed her palm against one and it flattened at her touch.

The wall rumbled and the small group tensed as it slid open to reveal a massive, brilliantly-lit cavern. A glittering crystal shone overhead, giving off light so bright that Victoria lifted her arm to shield her eyes.

"Welcome to New Fairhaven," Lady Spry said as the rumbling wall came to a stop.

Victoria peeked through her fingers to find a bustling city filled with stalls, makeshift homes, and at least two hundred elves and ogres. Everyone paused as the door opened, and they all stared at Victoria and her group with bated breath.

"It's Victoria!" someone shouted, breaking the silence.

Slowly a roar of voices built, and the hidden citizens of Fairhaven flocked toward the door. Victoria hesitated, not certain she could handle strangers coming at her, but Lady Spry stepped between Victoria and the onslaught of people.

"Back, please," she said in a loud and clear voice.

To Victoria's surprise, the citizens obeyed. They kept

their distance, but everyone continued to speak as Lady Spry led Victoria and her ragtag group of rebels into the hidden cavern. Once the last ogre had stepped through, the door rumbled closed behind them.

The voices overlapped each other, and Victoria could only catch snippets of each conversation.

"Mercy, it's really her—"

"—come to save us—"

"—knew she would—"

"—told you she wasn't dead! You owe me ten denni!"

She grimaced. *Great, now they're betting on whether or not I'm alive?*

"Miss Victoria?" a sweet little voice asked.

Victoria stopped in her tracks and looked down to find a young elvish girl, maybe six years old, hugging a tiny stuffed snarx as she stared up with wide eyes. Her little ears poked from her hair, too large for her head, and she had a dirt stain on her cheek.

Victoria knelt so that she would be eye-level with the little girl. "Yes?"

"Mommy says you're a hero. Are you here to help us, like she said?"

Victoria briefly scanned the crowd, but she didn't see any elvish women who looked like this kid. A twinge of sadness rocked her, and she wondered if her mother was in the dungeons, or worse. She forced as genuine a smile as she could muster and nodded. "I'm going to do what I can."

The girl sniffled, tears in the corner of her eyes, and Victoria panicked. *Fuck, crying kids.* She could take on a dungeon full of mercenaries and rip an enchanted door off its hinges, but she couldn't handle *this.*

"Hey, hey, cheer up," she said a bit nervously. She frantically looked around for help, but Audrey just shrugged. Diesel chuckled, and Edgar crossed his arms as he lifted one thick eyebrow in curiosity.

An idea sparked in the back of Victoria's mind, and she smiled gleefully. She pointed at Edgar. "Do you know who this is?"

Edgar stiffened. "What?"

The little girl nodded. "He's Captain of the Plits, your Berserk team."

"Dam…darn right," Victoria said, careful to censor herself in front of the kid. "How about he puts on a little show for you guys?"

"A what now?" Edgar asked dryly.

Victoria frowned at him and mouthed, "Go with it."

The big ogre rolled his eyes.

"A show?" the little girl asked.

"Yeah," Victoria said, standing. "The whole team will. We'll show you what Berserkers do to stay in shape and keep our minds sharp for the game. Anyone up for an impromptu Berserk match?"

The crowd roared, and the panicked faces relaxed ever so slightly. It was a distraction from the fear. A temporary one, but at least she could make them happy for a while.

In these tough times hope was their most valuable commodity, more precious than food. Hope could carry the rebels through the war, and Victoria would do anything in her power to keep them happy.

She grinned, scanning the crowd. "Who can show me to a decent Berserk field down here?"

CHAPTER ELEVEN

To be honest, Fyrn had to practically drag Victoria off the Berserk field. If it weren't for the war at hand she would have stayed there for days, chasing the elf and ogre children across the field instead of fidgets.

Gently, of course.

Besides, there weren't any bins on this makeshift Berserk field. She mostly just hoisted them over her head and ran around in circles for a bit before putting them down and chasing them again.

Great fun.

"Just five more minutes?" she whined as she followed her mentor to the designated war room. Two ogres stood at attention outside, their dented armor dull and lifeless, and both nodded to her as Fyrn pulled back the curtain so she could enter.

"Victoria, we have a dictator to kill. You can play with other people's kids later."

"Well, it's kind of creepy when you word it that way."

Fyrn shot a pointed look over his shoulder, and all Victoria could do was roll her eyes.

Ass.

An enchanted fire flickered in an improvised fireplace on the opposite wall, but no smoke clouded the room. Sconces along the walls lit the space well enough to see a map laid out on a crudely carved stone table in the center.

Several strangers lingered along the walls, including an elf who seemed vaguely familiar for reasons Victoria couldn't fully articulate. Styx sat on the ground by the fire, taking miniature bites out of an apple slice. Lady Spry, Audrey, Diesel, and Bertha stood around the table, and everyone tilted their heads toward Victoria as she entered. She nearly blushed with embarrassment at holding everyone up, but deep down she wasn't sorry.

She had needed a break, and she had given the rebels a bit of fun and hope amidst all the fear and suffering.

The familiar elf smiled warmly. "Thank you, Victoria, for giving them something to distract them from their pain."

"You did a good deed," Lady Spry said with a nod.

Victoria smiled. "My pleasure. Now, I believe we have a murderous Light Elf to kill?"

Audrey tapped her knuckle on the table. "Before we begin, I want to share that I infiltrated his army the other day."

Everyone shifted their gazes to her, the stunned silence almost painful.

"You did *what?*" Victoria snapped.

"I shifted form and became an elf, donned their uniform and listened in on their meeting. They didn't say anything useful, but I could continue doing it. You never know what we could learn."

Victoria gaped, sorting through too many angry retorts to pick one. "What the fuck were you thinking?" and "Are you completely insane?" were her current favorites.

"Why?" was all she managed.

Audrey lifted one eyebrow in confusion. "It's called 'spying.'"

"But... But Audrey, this is dangerous. Someone will recognize you. You could get caught."

"I got out, didn't I?"

"Yeah, but you went *once.*"

"I've been three times, actually, and no one has stopped me. They've leered a little bit, but I can handle myself."

Victoria set her hands on the table in an effort to suppress the scream growing in the back of her throat. "Audrey, you're going to get yourself captured, or worse, killed."

"He wouldn't kill her until he had you," Lady Spry said softly.

"Thanks, now I feel better," Victoria snapped.

Audrey crossed her arms. "Victoria, we need to have spies in this city listening to everything Luak's armies are doing. Lady Spry can only do so much. I'm helping how I can."

Victoria bit her cheek to keep from yelling at her best friend, who was only trying to help. "Please don't do that again, Audrey."

Audrey didn't answer.

"Has anyone stopped you?" Eldrin asked.

Audrey shook her head. "Like I said, nothing but leering

glances and a few snide remarks, but mostly I'm ignored. I listen in on the meeting and slip out after—easy. I blend in."

Her eyebrow twitched and Victoria caught the lie. With a frustrated sigh, she swallowed her pride. She would have to talk to Audrey about this later, since doing it in front of others would only make her more stubborn about it in the end.

Eldrin tapped the map with a finger as he absently scanned the city. "Luak's army must be growing more quickly than we anticipated if the captains don't recognize new recruits."

Lady Spry sighed deeply—the first time she had shown anything other than composed grace to Victoria—and rubbed her jaw. "Most likely, yes. He officially declared himself king today, and I'm certain he mobilized quite a force before doing so."

Audrey frowned. "Any bodies?"

"A few," the senator said. "Some of the military men have disappeared, those I suppose he had hoped would be more agreeable once promoted. I'm grateful to see that Lieutenant General Eldrin is alive and well." She nodded toward the familiar elf standing against the wall, who nodded somberly.

"Wait a minute!" Victoria said as it clicked for her. "Didn't I carry you out of the dungeon?"

Eldrin crossed his arms, chuckling. "That you did, my Lady, and I am forever in your debt."

In the aftermath of finding Fyrn on death's door, Victoria had admittedly lost track of Eldrin once they had returned to the house. He hadn't traveled with her group to the rebel area, so he must have used his connections to find the hideout on his own.

Diesel grinned. "Eldrin is an old friend of mine, and I couldn't let him rot in those dungeons even if he *does* cheat at cards."

A few of the soldiers and politicians in the war room laughed, and to his credit Eldrin merely shook his head in annoyance.

"We must focus," Fyrn said somberly from his place by the wall.

Everyone's smile fell, and Victoria set her hands on her hips. "He's right. How do we kill Luak?"

"*We* don't," Lady Spry said.

The room went silent, and every head in the room turned toward her. She, however, looked only at Victoria.

"You do," the regal woman finished.

"Laying it on a little thick there, huh?" Audrey asked with a raised eyebrow.

Victoria nudged her friend in the gut. "Audrey, come on."

"Well, she did."

Lady Spry frowned. "I apologize if my methods are dramatic, but I cannot stress this enough. Each of us hates Luak with a passion. He has stolen something dear from us all, robbed us of something beautiful, treasured, and irreplaceable. Each of us would like to be the one to deliver the fatal blow—whether via a sword to the gut or a spell to the head—but we can't. None of us are strong enough. Only you are, Victoria."

Victoria hesitated, her gaze drifting to the floor. She

didn't bother looking at Fyrn, even though she could feel the heat of his gaze on the back of her neck.

Maybe she wasn't.

"We need allies," the senator continued, scanning the faces around her. "More fighters. More soldiers. More denni to buy weapons and armor. More potions. We need friends with deep purses."

"I'll give what I can," Victoria said.

"As will I," Fyrn added.

"We all will," Diesel interjected, apparently not wanting to be one-upped by his adversary.

"However," Victoria said sharply, "we will *not* buy mercenaries."

Low murmurs erupted in the small room, but Victoria held her ground. Beside her, Audrey crossed her arms and squared her shoulders, backing Victoria up without a word.

"But Victoria, please—" Lady Spry began.

"No 'buts.' No mercenaries. Luak will just offer them more money, and there's a high chance they'll betray us."

"She's right," Eldrin said.

The room hushed, and Lady Spry stared blankly at the map. "But we need soldiers."

"I have a few ideas." Victoria rested her knuckles on the table, eyes roaming the map.

"The Berserk teams?" Audrey asked.

Victoria nodded. "All of them are fierce, ready to fight, and used to pain. They'll be valuable."

Lady Spry gestured to the curtain behind Victoria. "Most are here, but I've heard rumors of a few isolated pockets of rebels who haven't found this place yet. I will reach out to them."

"Good." Victoria tapped a familiar district near the outskirts of Fairhaven. "Out here, I have an old…friend, I guess you could call him. He may be useful."

Drefus, the Fairhaven crime boss she still owed a favor to. It was a risk, one she would have to discuss further with Fyrn. He knew the gremlin better than she did.

"No promises," she added.

"That's not enough," Eldrin said, resting his hands against the table.

Victoria smirked. She had saved the best for last. "I also have a friend in Lochrose. I believe the queen will join us."

The room went silent, every eye wide as they stared at her.

Lady Spry was breathless. "We heard you freed Lochrose, but to think they would help us after so long underground…"

"I can't promise anything, of course, but I may as well ask."

The senator's shoulders relaxed. "In that case, I believe we may stand a chance."

"I'm not convinced," Eldrin said, pointing to the various entrances to the castle. "Each of these doors is wide enough for five ogres to walk side by side, and the moment we attack we'll be swarmed.

"Then we let the castle protect itself," Lady Spry said.

"What?" Victoria stared at the woman, wondering what the hell that was supposed to mean.

"The castle's defenses are still active?" Fyrn asked incredulously.

Lady Spry shook her head. "Victoria, the castle itself is enchanted. It has a personality of its own, and it chooses its monarch. If its monarch is in trouble, it can cause a great deal of mayhem to whoever is trying to infiltrate its walls."

"If by 'trouble' you mean 'death,'" Fyrn muttered.

"How did I not know about this?" Diesel nearly shouted.

Fyrn chuckled. "I suppose the king didn't trust you with everything, hmm?"

Diesel frowned and crossed his arms, pouting.

Victoria chuckled. *A grown man pouting. How attractive!*

Lady Spry pursed her lips at the bickering wizards but pressed on. "The king was bound against speaking to anyone about it, Diesel. I maintain it, as did Fyrn for a time before, well..."

She glanced nervously at him, and the room went silent. Apparently Fyrn's banishment from the Order of the Silver Griffins was still a tense topic.

Lady Spry cleared her throat and continued, "We're part of a select few who knew about it before even King Bornt. Luak not only discovered it, but he also found a means of draining the castle's power to keep it obedient. It has been severely weakened, but I believe I can restore its strength. If not all of it, at least most."

"If you're capable of doing this, why didn't you do it sooner?" Fyrn asked.

Lady Spry sighed. "I debated it, but I don't think freeing the castle will be enough on its own. There are too many mercenaries, too much of the castle Luak still controls. I didn't discover his plot in time to help the castle keep him out. As much as I hate to admit it, Luak is painfully clever."

"But coupled with an attack on the castle, reactivating its defenses might be enough?" Victoria asked.

The senator shrugged. "Perhaps."

Victoria didn't like it. True, a castle coming alive could cause mayhem that would help in her attack on Luak's army, but she needed more. She needed something indestructible, something to draw Luak's attention without putting many—if any—lives at risk.

If only she had a secret weapon.

She tilted her head ever so slightly until she could see Fyrn out of the corner of her eye. He frowned, stiffening under her subtle scrutiny, and very slowly shook his head.

"Let's take a breather," Eldrin offered.

Diesel nodded. "Everyone, keep thinking about this. See if you have any other ideas."

One by one the attendees trickled out into the cavern, but Victoria gestured for Fyrn to stay. He walked over to the map, pretending to be consumed by it as everyone left.

In a moment only she, Audrey, and Fyrn remained.

"We have to, Fyrn," Victoria said, trying her best not to refer to the golems out loud.

He *had* sworn her to secrecy, after all.

"They aren't ready," he said softly.

Audrey laughed. "What? Do they need paint? This is an emergency!"

Fyrn frowned. "If I turned them on, they would be mindless killing machines with no master. I can power them and give them life, but I cannot make them obey. They are hardwired by magic to destroy anything in their path, and only a connection to something profound can direct their rage."

Victoria perked up. "Something profound? Like what?"

Fyrn sighed. "I don't know, that's the problem. The spell book says, 'Only a connection to something of profound power and will may control the minds of these granite assassins.' I've never found any more detail on what that could possibly mean."

Victoria groaned. *Great, back to Square One.*

CHAPTER TWELVE

Victoria once again stood in Drefus' lavish office. It hadn't changed a bit since she had come to him seeking the map to Atlantis, and if she were being honest, she hated the fact that she owed him a favor for traveling to a kingdom that had tried to kill her.

Assholes.

The elaborate room contrasted starkly with the drug den out front. A mahogany desk sat in the middle with a luxurious red carpet, and a fireplace roared behind it. Despite the fire, the room seemed cool and comfortable, as though the heat couldn't reach them.

As he always did, the short creature sat in his enormous chair, his seat raised so high that Victoria could see the leather cushion. Drefus was dressed in a suit, and his ears poked out on either side of the throne.

And, as always, he sneered. "What a pleasure to see you again, Victoria."

She suppressed a sarcastic huff as Fyrn closed the door

behind them. He had volunteered to join her in this endeavor, although he assumed it would fail.

To be honest, so did she. But she had to try.

"What can I do for you?" Drefus asked.

Victoria had toyed with her request the whole way here, but there simply wasn't a smooth way to word it. "We're going to kill Luak, and we want your soldiers."

The gremlin laughed and banged his tiny fist against the desk, apparently relishing the ridiculous request. He nodded to Fyrn. "She's straight to the point, isn't she?"

"I'm serious," Victoria snapped.

"I know you are," the gremlin said, sobering. "That's what makes it so damn funny."

She tried to hide her nerves with a defiant tilt of her chin. *Time to bluff him into compliance.* "Luak is stifling trade. There are fewer drug addicts in your den, Drefus, because there are fewer people in Fairhaven. The citizens are scared. They're leaving, or going underground. Your clientele is running away from you, and with them goes all your money. You're going to go broke, and it's Luak's fault. He'll squeeze every last penny from you and then leave you to rot."

"Will he, now?" The gremlin pressed his fingers together, grinning with a little too much glee. His eyes narrowed, and Victoria had a gut feeling that Drefus had had the privilege of speaking to Luak personally.

Damn it, he'd called her bluff.

The gremlin leaned on his elbows. "Victoria, the only reason I haven't called Luak to tell him you're here is because you still owe me a favor, and the potential gain from that favor outweighs the benefits of turning you in. If

Fyrn had come alone, he wouldn't have even made it to this room before he was captured."

Fyrn grunted in annoyance. Victoria, however, scowled with all the fury and hatred she could fit into one expression.

No one touched her friends.

"It's just business," the gremlin said with a shrug.

Victoria grimaced. "So that's it? You'll let him destroy Fairhaven?"

"Young lady, I benefit regardless of what happens to Fairhaven. This war is not my concern. Even if you win, you can't touch me." He opened a drawer and produced the coin that represented her favor to him.

She frowned. "Sorry I wasted your time."

The gremlin shrugged. "Don't let it happen again."

"I was talking to Fyrn," she said with a smirk.

As the sneer melted off Drefus' face, Victoria spun on her heel and stalked into the drug den, fuming.

Favor or no, she would take that little rat down—criminal empire and all.

Regina Spry knocked gently on the secret door that hid the castle's defense system.

After several seconds it slid open to reveal two elves, since ogres wouldn't have fit in this tiny space. They stared at her quizzically.

"What do you want, woman?" one of them asked crassly.

She suppressed an annoyed huff at the curt tone. "Hold this for me, won't you?"

She lifted one hand and laid it flat to reveal the powder in her palm. She quickly blew it into their faces and, within moments both stared blankly ahead.

The forgetfulness puff—it worked every time. She would have twenty minutes before the guards woke up, and another ten before they could remember anything.

Time to get to work.

She stepped into the small room, pushing the mercenaries against the walls as she climbed into the lone chair. They complied as though they were mannequins, just staring blankly ahead as she nudged them out of the way.

As she withdrew her wand from her sleeve, she muttered several ancient incantations. The tip of her wand glowed brilliantly green, and sparks of magic burst off the end. A shimmering portal appeared before her, rippling like a pond of molten gold, and the barest outline of a face hovered just out of reach in the puddle.

Dipping into the oldest spells she knew, she repeated her incantations until she could feel the distant tension of the drains Luak had placed on the castle. It was like pulling on taut ropes, and beads of sweat broke out along her hairline as she fought the powerful magic depleting her beloved palace.

One by one, the magical tendrils lifted, and with each release the face in the pool became clearer. She struggled, the minutes ticking away as she fought to free the castle, until the last thread finally slipped away.

The castle would be weak as it slowly regained its

power, but with time it would be even stronger than before.

Hate had that effect, after all.

A smooth face appeared in the pool, untouched by time or features. No lips, no eyes, no hair. It was more of a mask than a face, really, but it represented the castle all the same.

"My lovely Lady Spry, you have outdone yourself!" the castle boomed, its deep voice echoing in the tiny chamber.

She smiled and held a delicate finger to her lips. "We must be silent, Castle. They need to think you're still trapped."

"The indignity! Why would you ask such a thing? I can finally sense that wretched elf. I'll summon my saws—"

"No, Castle. You need time to recover. He has leeched much power from you, and he will win if you face him again so soon."

The castle huffed. "When do you propose we attack, then? I have no king to give me orders anymore."

Regina sighed. "Bornt is dead."

The mask in the golden pool nodded. "Indeed. I no longer feel his presence anywhere."

Regina sniffled, heart sinking at the loss of her friend. "Aren't you sad? You knew him his entire life, ever since he was a boy."

"My Lady, I am a castle. I feel only victory and rage."

Through her loss, she couldn't help but chuckle. With a glance over her shoulder, she wiped away a tear and tried to focus. "Your new queen will be here soon. We need to make it possible for her to take her rightful place."

"And who is this woman? What makes you think she is worthy?"

Regina smiled warmly. "You'll see, Castle. She's perfect."

"I will at least meet her, Lady Spry, but only since you seem fond of her. May I remind you that *I* choose my monarch, not the other way around."

"Of course. I'll call for you soon, but for now I'll place a false screen over your mask to make them think you're still being drained. Please, Castle, I beg you not to act until I return."

"And if you don't? If Luak kills you before you can come to me?"

Lady Spry hesitated, considering their options. "Then Luak is yours to do with as you please. If he kills me, let all hell break loose."

"I was right to like you," the castle said.

Regina waved her wand, summoning the cloaking spell that would fool Luak's guards—and hopefully Luak himself. She stood, and slipped out the door with only moments to spare before the guards regained their senses.

She hurried down the hall to her bedchamber, content with their plan thus far. It contained far too many what-ifs for her liking, but at least the resistance finally *had* a plan.

She would do everything in her power to see that Luak failed.

CHAPTER THIRTEEN

"You want me to do *what?*" Queen Angelique of Lochrose paused mid-bite, a half-eaten croissant dangling from her delicate fingers she stared at Victoria with an utterly baffled expression.

"I know it's a lot to ask, Angelique," Victoria said, glancing around the Lochrose palace. They sat in the same dining hall where Victoria had first met Angelique what felt like years ago, but which had been mere weeks.

Just a handful of weeks since she had faced the sphinx, and she was already back to ask for a favor.

Only the two of them sat at the massive banquet table, a modest array of cheeses and breads set before them to whet their appetites while they discussed politics and war. Styx helped himself to most of the food on Victoria's plate, mumbling happily as he gorged.

Audrey had stayed in the hidden tunnels to strategize, and Fyrn was off buying some rare potion that could only be found here. Since he had created the illegal portal that had gotten them here so quickly, he was Victoria's ticket home.

After she got Angelique to agree to join their war, of course.

"Victoria, it's more than 'a big ask.' You're requesting that my people die for you." Angelique leaned back in her chair, food forgotten as she processed the appeal.

Victoria sighed. "I wouldn't be asking unless I absolutely needed your help. Fairhaven is being overrun, and every time I leave it gets worse. More people die. More people disappear. More homes are burned to the ground. He's taking over my home city, Angelique. Surely you can understand what that's like."

Angelique's jaw tensed, and her gaze flitted to the floor.

Victoria leaned across the table, choosing each word as carefully as she could so as not to lose what progress she had made. "We don't know who will be king when the dust settles, but I can promise you this—you will have a powerful ally in whoever rules next. Fairhaven will be forever in your debt, forever your friend when you need us. You're reemerging in the magical world after being lost to the ages, and you're going to face growing pains as con artists and mercenaries come here to make their fortunes. We can help each other, Angelique. Always."

Angelique smiled ruefully, softly shaking her head as she made her decision. "You present quite the argument, Victoria Brie."

She shrugged modestly. "I say it like it is."

"That you do. How would we even find you?"

"With this." Victoria pulled out a roll of parchment.

"What is it?"

"An enchanted map, courtesy of Fyrn. This will lead you to us and includes the counter spells to the protections we've put around our camp. If we move, this will show you where we've gone."

The Queen frowned deeply. "That's a dangerous map to have made. In the wrong hands…"

"If you accept and help us, this map will only work for you."

The Queen sighed and tapped a thin finger on her chin, eyes shifting out of focus as she internally debated everything Victoria had shared thus far.

"So what will it be?" Victoria asked softly.

Angelique caught Victoria's eye, and the concerned frown bled away into a gentle smile. "Very well, my friend. For you, anything. It will take some time, but we will assemble our army."

Victoria sighed with relief. "Thank you, Angelique. Oh my God, thank you."

Angelique chuckled. "Don't thank me yet. Keep in mind that my soldiers haven't trained to fight anything but a single monster. We will need guidance from your military leaders on what to expect and how to prepare."

"How long will you need?"

"A month."

Victoria let out the tiniest of panicked moans, trying her best not to be ungrateful. "I don't know if we have a month."

"Then I apologize, but we cannot move faster. We need not only to mobilize our army, but also train them to fight new foes. A month is fast, seeing as we are utterly unprepared to fight a Rhazdon host as powerful as you say this Luak person is."

"You're right." Victoria leaned her elbows on the table, trying to calm her racing heart. This was still a win, even if it put her pulse into overdrive.

Would they arrive in time? She simply didn't know.

Angelique set a graceful hand on top of Victoria's. "Remember, my friend, that these witches and wizards have never fought a real war in their lives. What we do for you, we do to repay the freedom you gave us. We need time to make sure we do it properly."

Victoria nodded and forced a smile, one she hoped seemed genuine. These witches and wizards weren't really soldiers. They were recently-freed prisoners who had no idea what life was like outside of Lochrose, and yet they still rallied to her defense.

As her mind raced with possibilities of how to delay Luak a month, her heart sank into her stomach as she realized she might have just signed these good people's death warrants.

CHAPTER FOURTEEN

Once more disguised as a Light Elf, Audrey pressed herself against the wall in the mercenaries' assembly hall. Dozens of ogres and elves congregated, arguing with each other or sharpening their blades as they waited for the captain to arrive.

During the last week, Audrey had slipped into the meeting hall whenever she could. The resistance needed as much information as they could gather, and she possessed a unique ability that could get them that information.

Even if Victoria hated that her friend slipped away to do this, Audrey didn't feel like she had a choice. It was a risk, sure, but it had already paid off. They knew patrol routes, times, the size of Luak's army—incredibly valuable intel.

But lately, more eyes drifted to her as she entered. More gazes lingered. More heads tilted toward each other, whispering as they watched her lean against the back wall.

She glared at one pair of orcs who stared openly at her, waiting for them to look away.

They didn't.

Her jaw tensed. Perhaps she *had* been pushing her luck. Maybe they had begun to notice the Light Elf no one seemed to recognize, the one who always hung out near the door.

Last in, first out. That was Audrey's way to stay safe and give herself an escape route should she need it—and it was starting to look like she might.

Shoulders tensed, legs itching to run, Audrey eyed the door. Maybe it was time to go. If she was subtle, possibly she could just slip out without anyone stopping her. Wait for a distraction and then—

"Shut the doors," a booming voice ordered from somewhere in the crowd.

Shit. She gulped, trying to relax her shoulders as she panicked internally.

As the doors creaked shut to begin the meeting, the massive ogre who often spoke to the troops pushed through the crowd and jumped onto the platform. She would have to wait this one out.

The soldiers fell silent as the ogre paced the platform, hands behind his back as his gaze drifted from face to face in the crowd. It seemed almost like he was looking for someone, and Audrey gritted her teeth with nerves.

You're being paranoid, she chided herself.

I do not think you are, the koi said in her mind.

Not helping. Not. Helping.

Please find an exit, the koi prodded. *I've grown rather fond of you and would prefer it if you did not die today.*

Audrey rolled her eyes. *Thanks for the warm fuzzies. Focus!*

Audrey scanned the walls as the orc continued to pace the raised platform, but the only other door was on the opposite end of the room. It stood open, like a beacon inviting her to freedom, but she knew better. It led into the castle, toward Luak. Besides, she couldn't move through a stationary crowd without being seen. It was better to wait for the meeting to adjourn.

The ogre's eyes rested on her and he sneered. "There you are."

Nope, change of plans. She would *not* be waiting for the meeting to adjourn.

"Grab her!" the ogre shouted. The crowd surged toward her, and the nearest elves reached for her neck.

With her cover blown, Audrey didn't bother keeping the elf form. She needed her Atlantean magic to fight, since she couldn't do much of anything as an elf. Her body hummed and shimmered as it returned to its natural state, and she lifted one hand in front of her. The other she shoved into her pocket, grabbing the Atlantean gem hidden in her clothes.

Her hands brimmed with white energy, the electricity rolling over her skin like lightning. Several of the nearest soldiers shrank away, apparently not certain what she was doing, and her threat kept the crowd at bay.

For the moment, anyway.

If she wanted out of here, she would have to keep the upper hand. That meant acting first and staying on the offensive.

It also meant blowing shit up.

Audrey turned her attention to the door, and in a matter of seconds blew it apart with her brilliant white magical energy. Splintered boards rained on the crowd, and while they ducked she ran.

She bolted through the hallway, shooting rays of white light at anyone in her path. Some of the elves jumped out of the way or pressed themselves against the wall, but many tried to attack her. She dodged sword after sword, fist after fist, and spell after spell while she raced for the exit.

With every burst of magic from her hands, she wondered if this was it. She was facing an army by herself with only the now-lost element of surprise on her side.

Worst of all, she had to admit Victoria was right. She should never have done this.

Back home in the protected tunnels, Victoria leaned over the Fairhaven map in their war room. She bit her lip as she pored over what she knew of the remaining families, wondering which—if any—would be willing to help.

The flutter of tiny wings caught her attention, and she glanced as a fairy bolted through the cloth covering the doorframe. The little male huffed, wheezing as he waved for her attention.

"Yes?" she asked, a little confused by the interruption.

"Audrey…castle. Hurry…" he wheezed.

Victoria frowned, heart thudding as she processed the fairy's warning. Audrey had infiltrated the meeting hall again, and this time they had caught her.

"Where?" Victoria demanded.

"South side, near the town square," the fairy said, finally catching his breath.

Victoria charged through the door, running toward the exit. Portals took time to create, time she didn't have. She had to run, and even if she did she might not get there in time.

Four elves and two ogres blocked the barred doors as Audrey sprinted toward the exit. This was the final door—her salvation—and she would make it through.

With the last of her magic, she shot a brilliant bolt of white light at the guards. Some of them jumped out of the way, but most were thrown into the massive doors, which burst open and sprinkled shards of wood and metal on the cobblestone streets outside.

She raced into the brilliant light from the overhead crystals, sucking in deep breaths of victory and relief as she bolted through the street. A tunnel in the nearby alley would take her back to—

Something hit her square in the back. The force knocked her over, and she rolled several feet. When her body finally stopped, she groaned. Every inch of her ached, and searing pain shot up her leg. She tried to stand, but agony splintered through her shoulder. Whatever had hit her had broken several bones.

Grimacing, she glared back the way she had come to find a familiar elf sneering at her as he slowly approached, all but swaggering through the street.

"Hello, little Atlantean," Luak said.

Audrey tried to stand, to push through the pain, but she fell again onto her stomach. Dirt and blood covered her hands, her arms—probably everything. Her tousled hair hid much of the world around her from view, but all she cared about was Luak.

"I'm afraid I've forgotten your name," he said, chuckling. "I usually refer to you as 'the sidekick.'"

Her anger getting the better of her, Audrey reached for the crystal in her pocket. Luak, fast as lightning, shot a fireball at her side, driving her backward from the sheer force of the blow. More bones broke as she rolled, and she stifled a scream of agony.

He clicked his tongue in disappointment. "You come uninvited into my home, destroy much of my barracks, and have the audacity to try to attack me?"

"It's not your home," she spat.

"Oh, but it is."

He lifted Audrey by the collar, and her entire body screamed with pain as he shifted broken bones that were not meant to be touched. He chuckled, no doubt relishing her suffering.

"You'll make excellent bait to draw out Victoria," he said, his face inches from hers. "Let's make sure you put on a proper performance though, hmm? Scream for me."

"Kiss my ass."

He chuckled and, instead of answering he grabbed her broken forearm. She bit back a shriek and her body recoiled at his touch, the agony threatening to tear its way out of her throat.

"Come now," he said gently, as though helping a child learn to walk. "You're almost there."

Time slowed as he held her in the air, suspended and biting back tears. But with a sudden, violent shift, the mood changed. One moment, his hand on her collar sent ripples of pain throughout her body, and the next a stranger's fist had collided with his cheek. He flew across the street and Audrey dropped, suddenly unsupported.

Two powerful arms caught her. She looked up to see Victoria glaring at a pile of bricks as Luak climbed out of the hole he had dug in the street. She winked at Audrey.

"Thanks, Superman," Audrey slurred, the pain too much to bear.

Victoria's brows tilted upward in concern, and she raced toward a nearby alley. "Fyrn's slow as hell, so Diesel is coming. He'll get you out of here."

"But you—"

"I'm fine." Victoria smiled briefly and returned to the street as Audrey huddled in the shadows, sick and horrified at what she had done.

Victoria wasn't ready to face Luak. Not now.

Not yet.

Victoria and Luak didn't banter. No need… Each had what each other wanted, and all they cared about was taking what was theirs.

Luak wanted Victoria's Rhazdon Artifact, and Victoria wanted Fairhaven. Neither would get what they wanted until the other was dead.

Their battle raged, and Victoria lost track of time. No nearby buildings survived her impact when Luak's fist connected with her body. No structure survived the crackling rage of his fire.

And *no* one dared come close to the carnage.

After a sharp blow to her chest Victoria sailed backward and rolled in the cobblestone road. She finally slid to a stop, focusing all her energy on the Rhazdon Artifact that would heal her while she summoned her bear figurine's sheer force of will to keep going.

She didn't know how long she and Luak had been fighting, but half her clothes were singed off and Luak's broken jaw gave him an almost comical appearance as he stalked toward her. He likely wished he had a wizard medic handy, but she wouldn't give him a breather long enough to use one.

His army surrounded them, no doubt waiting for the order to attack, but his pride had kept him from it. That, or the fear they would take the Artifact if she died—Victoria couldn't be sure.

But with every blow, he pushed her farther down the street. He broke her bones, split her skin, hit her hard enough for her to see stars.

He was ruthless. And she...

She wasn't strong enough.

As her body healed yet again, she stumbled toward him. Even with all her strength, even with her healing powers, even with the massive sword and shield she could summon at will...

Luak was winning.

The Light Elf raised his hands, palms outstretched, and fire erupted along his skin. His magic had already burned her so many times that she knew how he would attack—

one hand to her head, the other to her chest. If she didn't raise her shield in time, it would hurt. Badly. She would be thrown into the air and she would hit something hard, and probably break another bone—or five.

She gritted her teeth, wishing this was like tackling ogres. She didn't fully understand the magic in Luak's Rhazdon Artifacts, but it was enough to defeat even her new power.

Sure enough, the swirl of fire surged at her. She summoned her shield, but it appeared one second too late.

Her skin charred, black and bubbling as his attack threw her backward and she hit something hard. As she sank to the ground, her vision blurred, edges darkening, and she desperately tried to keep her head upright.

"Stay awake," she muttered to herself.

Victoria pushed herself to her feet, but she swayed and the world spun as a fiery blur stalked toward her from afar. Hand outstretched, she ran into a wall. Bricks crumbled under her palm, and she cussed loudly.

"Stay awake," she told herself again.

She fell to her knees, the force of her fall denting the cobblestone road. Her hands hit the street as she fought to retain her balance, but she couldn't.

She just couldn't.

Her body collapsed onto the ground, her bear's will shattered and her body too broken to heal. With a last shaky breath, her world went dark.

CHAPTER FIFTEEN

When Victoria finally came to, she bolted upright with her fists at the ready.

She blinked rapidly as she tried to clear her blurry vision, and it took several tries before she could make out the hazy outline of a four-poster bed and a window. Someone was hunched in a chair by the door, and she leapt out of the bed before the final blurry elements of the world around her came into focus. Fists cocked, she was ready to pick up where she'd left off.

"Victoria, it's me!" Diesel yelled.

The man in the chair stood, and Diesel's familiar face came into focus.

"Oh, thank goodness," she said, leaning against the mattress as she calmed down. Her world still spun, and her head throbbed.

Diesel held her tightly, pressing her head against his chest. His pulse thudded erratically against her ear, and she couldn't help but smile with gratitude at his worry.

Worry. Wait, I should be worried about... About...

As her mind cleared, she straightened and grabbed his shirt. "Audrey! She's in an alley and she needs help!"

"She's safe," he said gently, hands on Victoria's shoulders. "Sleeping. She doesn't have instant healing like you do. Fyrn healed her himself, but she will be out for a while."

Victoria sighed deeply and sat on the bed, head in her hands as she tried to calm down. "I lost."

Diesel perched on the bed beside her and put an arm around her shoulders, squeezing gently as he held her. "You lasted longer than most would have."

"That's not good enough."

He sighed. "At least you survived."

"How, though? He'd knocked me out cold."

Diesel flashed a cocky smile. "I rescued you."

She laughed. "I'm never going to live that one down, am I?"

"Not in a million years. I will forever be the one who rescued the fair Victoria Brie in her time of need. So effectively, when you save Fairhaven *I* should get the most credit since I saved your life."

She rolled her eyes. "Thank you, Diesel."

His smile fell, and he tilted her shoulders toward him. Still reeling from the battle with Luak, she didn't resist. He hesitated, his eyes darting between hers and the floor as he searched for what he wanted to say.

She set a hand on his chest to stop him from saying a word. "You want me to not face him again, but you know I will. You want to save me, but know I don't need saving. You're trying to show me how much you care without annoying the living crap out of me."

"Maybe," he admitted.

With a chuckle, Victoria stood and rubbed her aching neck. Her Rhazdon Artifact must have worked overtime to mend everything in her body. She suspected most people would have died from a fight like that. In fact, she was likely one of the few who had walked away from a battle with Luak.

Lost in thought, she paced the room. "He *must* have a weakness—something I can use against him."

"Just rest, Victoria. You need to heal."

"I *am* healing. I need to figure out how to kill Luak before he gets any stronger."

"He's not—"

"New troops every day. Bottomless pockets and a rich benefactor. And after that fight, he'll probably realize he needs a bit more power to beat me. I can't let him win, Diesel."

"Even if you die?" He stood up, a good foot taller than her as he stepped closer. For the first time, his expression twisted into one of anger.

He was mad…at her. Victoria had to admit she had never thought she would see the day, but in this he was wrong.

"Yes, Diesel," she said softly. "Even if I die."

His brows twisted upward and he reached for her shoulders again, but this time he couldn't bring himself to touch her, so his hands hovered an inch from her skin. She watched him, waiting for him to tell her to stop and rethink this, but he didn't. After a moment, he just nodded. "That's what makes you a hero, Victoria."

"Diesel, look—"

The door burst open and Fyrn stood in the doorway.

He lifted one hairy eyebrow at the scene, and Diesel stepped back without another word.

"I told you to come get me when she woke up," Fyrn said.

Diesel crossed his arms. "We had things to discuss first. A lover's quarrel, if you will. Our first, I might add!"

"Oh my God, Diesel," Victoria muttered. She shook her head, pinching the bridge of her nose.

At least he was back to his old self—no more anger. He knew what she was willing to do to protect those in her beloved city, and not even he could stop her.

No one could.

For Fairhaven and for justice, she would do what needed to be done.

"We have to talk," Fyrn said with a nod to the hallway. "Come with me."

"He nearly killed you," Fyrn said as they settled into couches.

Victoria sipped a warm cup of tea, savoring the wispy heat radiating from the liquid. There weren't many places of comfort in their rocky hideaway, but the refugees had managed to sneak out a few nice-ish things. The checkered green couch she sat on had seen better days, and a few threads of the overstuffed cushions tickled the inside of her knee as she fought to get comfortable.

"Luak's stronger than I realized," Victoria admitted. It was her way of agreeing without admitting it outright.

"You need more power," Fyrn said with a disgusted

grunt. He reclined in the cracked brown leather armchair that reminded her somewhat of his chair back at his house. By now his home had probably been ransacked.

From his chair by the smokeless fire, Diesel quirked an eyebrow. "*More* power? She's a freaking superhero, Fyrn. How much more magic can you shove into a human's body?"

Victoria absently tapped a finger on her chin as she debated her options. She kept coming back to one, but she didn't like it.

Not one bit.

Diesel stood and started pacing. "So what do we do, protection spells? You think I haven't done a million of those already?"

Victoria tilted her head. "You've been performing magic on me without telling me?"

"Of course, my darling. I need to make sure luck is on your side, after all. A few prosperity potions in your tea, a victory and triumph charm or two. Nothing major."

Fyrn chuckled. "Those spells would have cost your entire fortune, Victoria, if this idiot wasn't absolutely enamored with you. They were quite good."

"Hey, I... Thank you?" Diesel seemed confused as to whether to address the insult or the rare compliment first.

"Hold on, how did I not know you were performing *magic* on me? That's kind of a big deal!"

"It was for your safety, my darling."

"It... Well, yeah, and thank you, but what if other people are performing magic on me too? This is—"

"You're fine, Victoria," Fyrn interrupted. "We've placed

wards to keep other wizards' charms and magic off you as much as possible."

"Well, *telling me* would have been nice." She rubbed her face. Freaking wizards. *Always doing magic without telling me anything.*

At least this was in her favor.

"So there aren't any more spells we can do," Diesel said, rubbing the stubble on his jaw.

"No amulets or small magical tokens would be powerful enough," Fyrn added.

Victoria eyed Fyrn's staff. "What about an artifact and a relic fused together?"

Both wizards paused in their thoughts and stared at her —Diesel with concern and Fyrn with surprise.

"Wielding a powered artifact is incredibly dangerous," Diesel said.

"The only two relics powerful enough to defeat Luak are…" Fyrn glanced at his staff and then at Victoria, and she pieced it together.

The only two relics Fyrn knew of either powered his staff or had been put aside to power the golems.

Victoria sipped her tea, her gaze drifting to Diesel. "May I speak with Fyrn alone for a moment?"

The younger wizard sighed. "Of course. I'll go…scout something."

"Thank you."

When the door had shut softly behind him, Victoria gestured toward it—someone might overhear them. Fyrn had the same idea, and as he had when they had visited Drefus in his drug den, he summoned a glimmering bubble of silence. No one outside the bubble would hear anything said inside.

"It's a solid idea," she said.

"It would be if you knew more about powered artifacts."

"Then enlighten me."

"My staff keeps me alive, Victoria, but I trained for decades to master its power. Relics and artifacts as powerful as this can be erratic, and if you're unprepared they can overwhelm and destroy you when you try to control their power. It takes years to master one, and that's time we don't have."

She let out a disappointed sigh. "And the golems?"

"They can be used if we can find a means of controlling them. The power of the relic fueling them will be diluted since there are many golems, and it won't overwhelm whoever controls them."

"So we just have to find this 'connection to something profound' to control them."

"It's too vague. We can't awaken them unless we're certain the connection to this…thing, whatever it is, is powerful enough."

Victoria stood with a frustrated huff, pacing the small bubble as best she could. "We have to do *something*. Our little spat in the town square proves I can't defeat him on my own, at least not yet. When we face him, everyone else will fight his army but I'll face *him*, and this time I can't lose."

"I know," Fyrn said softly.

An idea hovered just out of reach in the back of her mind. It was an infuriating sensation, same as she had felt earlier when training with Audrey and Fyrn. This was one of her new powers, and the one she perhaps understood the least. With her bear figurine she had access to intuitive knowledge and understanding of the world around her, but she didn't quite know how to use it yet.

Frustrating, to say the least.

She did, however, have one idea on her own.

"I should find another Rhazdon Artifact," she said softly.

He sighed with disappointment. Apparently he'd had this idea, too.

"Is there one that would help me?"

"There are dozens that would help you," Fyrn said. "And dozens more that would turn you into what Luak is now."

"I'm obviously not like him, Fyrn. I have two Rhazdon Artifacts already, and I'm fine."

"Absolute power corrupts absolutely," he said, quoting Lord Acton.

"You yourself said that I needed more power," she pointed out.

"I know." He rubbed his forehead, frustrated.

"With my bear figurine, I have the force of will and discipline to overcome any temptation that may come with whatever Rhazdon Artifact we choose. I'll also be able to keep its ghost in line."

"Is that what you want to do every day for the rest of your life?"

"If it means protecting Fairhaven, yes!"

Fyrn watched her for a moment, the lines around his eyes betraying his age. He looked weathered and deeply weary.

"If anyone can handle three Rhazdon Artifacts, it's you," he said.

She smiled, grateful for the compliment. "If you're going to keep saying nice things to people, they're going to wonder if you're losing your mind."

He chuckled, rubbing his beard. "I suppose they will. I'm the old fart, after all. Can't go around giving compliments."

She laughed. "It just wouldn't be right."

"Very well." He stood and dismissed the golden light protecting them with a wave of his hand, and the magic shield popped like a bubble landing on the point of a needle.

"Don't we get a say in this?" a familiar male voice said from behind her.

Victoria spun on her heel to find Shiloh leaning against the wall. Elle draped her arms over the back of the couch Victoria had been sitting on, and both watched her.

"I'd like a new friend. I bet they'll be nicer than you," Elle hopped onto the couch and reclined, stretching her legs. The tiny ghost barely filled the length of the couch.

"Maybe they'll keep you from bugging me all the time." Shiloh inspected his nails, bored as ever, and Victoria couldn't help but wonder where the ghosts went when they weren't around her. It seemed as though Elle didn't bother Shiloh a bit, but there was likely more going on than met the eye.

With magic, there always was.

"I guess it's settled, then," Victoria said with an amused shake of her head. That was easy.

Besides, they couldn't stop her.

Shiloh lifted his chin as though he had read her mind, and their eyes locked. "Let me remind you, Victoria, that we are mild compared to many of the ghosts tied to Rhazdon Artifacts. Before I was bound to mine, I saw the sort of...*people*...Rhazdon chose for this magic. Some would actively lead their hosts to death out of vengeance for being trapped, and others will torment you night and day in hopes you'll end yourself. Not all ghosts are good."

"That's enough, Shiloh," Fyrn snapped.

The ghost shrugged. "It's true. There's one nearby."

"There's—wait, you can sense other Rhazdon Artifacts?" Victoria stood up taller.

He nodded toward Elle. "So can she, but she's too loud and obnoxious to notice."

Elle pouted, arms crossed. "You are so mean!"

Victoria stepped between them, trying to settle their little spat. "Guys? Guys! Focus."

"There is in fact another Rhazdon Artifact nearby," Fyrn said. "Sort of."

"Where?"

"In the bowels of Fairhaven."

Victoria set her hands on her hips. "You mean there was a Rhazdon Artifact *here* and you sent me to Sedona to kill a sphinx?"

"Hey!" Elle said.

Victoria glanced at the little elf girl. "I'm grateful to have you, little one. I am."

Elle smiled.

Fyrn stared into the fire. "This one wouldn't have given you the strength you needed to wield your sword and shield. Its powers are largely unknown, save for one —divination."

"What does that mean?"

"The future is fluid, changing every moment, but you will have the power to see what is coming for you. I believe this will help you instinctively avoid danger in a fight. You will see the blow seconds before it hits you, so Luak will not be able to hurt you unless you let him."

Victoria grinned. "If he can't hit me, I can kill him."

"Precisely. But it comes at a cost."

She rolled her eyes. "Doesn't it always?"

"The ghost tied to this Artifact is truly insane. Legend has it she was unhinged before she was killed for the Rhazdon Artifact, but the process broke her. She will actively try to get you killed every minute of every day. You must never listen to her."

"Lovely." Victoria looked at her ghosts. They were crazy, but they were the fun kind of crazy. "Having a psycho killer in the family would really balance us out, don't you think, guys?"

"You're hilarious," Shiloh said dryly.

"Where is this Rhazdon Artifact, Fyrn?"

He sighed. "In the deepest tunnels of Fairhaven, where even I don't go. But for you—for this—I will."

An involuntary shiver raced down Victoria's spine. If even Fyrn wouldn't go there, it must be a truly dark place.

"It sounds like we should get a team together," Victoria said.

Fyrn nodded. "Audrey should wake within a week or two, and Diesel should join us, but aside from those two we should go alone. The tunnels are filled with dangerous things, and a large group would get lost."

Victoria nodded. "Works for me."

"In the meantime, I need to research what's down there."

"Are you sure the Rhazdon Artifact is there?"

He nodded. "I'm many things, Victoria, but I'm not reckless. I've spent my life researching the Rhazdon Artifacts, and I know where many are. I've cross-referenced enough printed and handwritten knowledge to know it's there. I simply need to verify a few things before we head down, which will take some time."

She frowned. "We don't have long, Fyrn."

"I understand, but I cannot put you at further risk. It's asking too much of you. When we go, we will be prepared."

Smiling, she set a hand on her mentor's shoulder. "Thank you."

"Of course. But Victoria?"

"Yes?"

"This will be your last Rhazdon Artifact." Instead of a forceful or commanding expression, he watched her with a flicker of hope.

He was asking, in his own weird way.

"I'll do what I have to."

Other Rhazdon hosts might have been fueled by an insatiable desire for power and control, but Victoria was different. She just wanted enough power to protect her new home—the only home she had left, thanks to Luak.

And this time her home wouldn't burn to the ground with everyone she loved trapped inside.

CHAPTER SIXTEEN

Audrey's head was killing her.

She grimaced and sat upright in bed, gingerly holding her forehead as she tried to focus on something—anything—in the blurry room around her.

The soft light streaming through the window was the first thing to come into focus. The gentle beams fell on the bumps in her comforter. Her arm rested in her lap, and the skin was covered in deep purple bruises.

Fragments of what had happened swam through her mind: Luak chasing her, fire, Victoria's calm smile as she came to the rescue.

Victoria.

Dread shot through her and she scrambled to stand. A dizzy spell put her back on the mattress, but she pushed through it and stumbled to the door. With an unbalanced yank, she swung open the door and all but fell into the hallway.

"Victoria!"

Down the hall, something crashed and splintered. Feet

shuffled over the floor, and a familiar pixie shot out of a room, fists raised and ready to fight. Seconds later, a redhead appeared in the doorway. "Audrey? What happened?"

"Oh, thank goodness," Audrey leaned against the wall, holding her head again as her world swam. Her disorientation was kind of like being drunk, but without the fun and heady high that usually came with it.

"Hey, calm down! It's okay." Victoria put one of Audrey's arms around her shoulders and led her back into the bedroom.

"What happened?" Audrey asked.

"You've been out for a few days."

"Did you beat Luak?"

Victoria chuckled. "Not quite. Here, sit down. We have a lot to talk about."

An hour later, Victoria lounged in the same sitting area she had shared with Fyrn a week earlier while they discussed what to do next. She sat in silence, watching Audrey process everything. So far all Audrey had done was stare into her tea.

"Are you sure this is a good idea?" Audrey asked.

Victoria shrugged. "I'm not a fan of having a ghost that wants to kill me, but this power will be useful. It's the final piece of the puzzle, Audrey."

"I trust you, V. If you want to do this, I'll back you up. When do we leave?"

"As soon as you're ready."

Audrey stood, wobbling a bit. "I'm ready."

Victoria chuckled. "Not even close. Eat. Heal. Rest up. Fyrn did what he could, but you were in a bad state. You need to regain your strength first, maybe get in a few more healing sessions before we leave."

"But you need time to train with this new Rhazdon Artifact."

"Yeah, and I need to make sure we all get there in one piece, too. Every second counts, but that doesn't mean we should rush blindly into a deadly new adventure. Go stuff your face."

Audrey chuckled. "Doctor's orders?"

Victoria held open the door. "Yep. Before we face certain death, let's go eat a shitload of junk food."

"Best doctor ever."

"You know it."

While Audrey rested and let herself heal, Victoria played Berserk.

Of course, it wasn't *real* Berserk, considering they didn't have a field or fidgets, but it was a pleasant way to burn off energy nonetheless.

Victoria built up a bit of a routine for herself as the days blurred by: grab some stew and bread from the kitchens, answer the incessant questions of the gaggle of children that followed her to her table, and then race them to their makeshift Berserk field.

Over the past weeks new refugees had begun to trickle in, many of them Berserk players, both professional and not. Between matches, she lost track of the lines of ogres who wanted to be tossed over her head like ragdolls. She would absolutely *have* to find Edgar and tell him to friggin' stop telling people about that.

And everywhere she went, people smiled with hope.

Each smile reminded her of the life they had abandoned, the life Luak had stolen from them all. He had taken their freedom and forced them to hide, but through it all they never forgot to seek laughter and joy. Even in a barren retreat deep in the monster-filled caves below the city, the tenacious people of Fairhaven would not be broken.

Nor would she. Everything she did was for them.

For Fairhaven.

For home.

Two weeks after Audrey woke up, Fyrn finally said she was ready to go with them into Fairhaven's deepest tunnels.

"About freaking time," Audrey muttered. "I was ready a week ago."

"It astounds me that someone could be more hard-headed than Victoria," Fyrn grumbled.

"Hey, leave me out of this." Victoria adjusted the strap on her pack. Because it had been filled with enough food and water to last them weeks, the bag had been passed to the strongest of them.

Glorified pack-mule, basically.

Diesel lifted the pack off Victoria's shoulders, but it nearly hit the floor. "Good gracious, my love, do you have bricks in here?"

She chuckled and lifted it effortlessly onto her back. Its weight was nothing to her thanks to her bear's magic, but she appreciated the gesture nonetheless.

Styx flitted up to her, a tiny backpack on his shoulders as he grinned proudly. Victoria smiled, grateful for her pixie's courage. "I need you to stay here."

His smile fell.

"I'm sorry, buddy, but this is dangerous stuff. Besides, someone has to protect all the refugees. Think you can handle that?"

He puffed out his tiny chest and saluted before flying off down the hall. Victoria chuckled, grateful the little guy would be out of harm's way. If these tunnels scared even Fyrn, she would have to be at the top of her game—and she couldn't risk Styx getting hurt.

Diesel ran a hand through his hair. "I've been researching these tunnels, Fyrn, and they're bad news."

"Obviously. They're supposed to keep treasure hunters away from powerfully dark magic."

"But the defenses down there…" He shuddered.

Victoria frowned. "What's down there?"

"We don't know much, darling," Diesel admitted, putting a hand on her shoulder.

She shrugged it off with a chuckle. "Diesel, focus and tell me what you *do* know."

"Very little. No one has gone very far and lived to return."

"Oh, awesome," Audrey muttered.

"A few journals have been discovered, some detailing wonderful riches and treasures in rooms no one else has ever found. They mention voices guiding them to the greatest piles of gold and denni they've ever seen, and then the entries just stop. Some in the rescue parties have heard singing or enchanting voices urging them deeper into the tunnels, but they didn't dare follow."

Fyrn tapped his staff on the ground. "They're sirens."

Victoria almost laughed. "Sirens? Like, the lead-you-to-your-death kind?"

"Aren't those in the oceans, though?" Audrey asked.

"Some are, yes," Fyrn said.

"How do we have sirens in the tunnels below Fairhaven?" Victoria asked.

"Sirens live by a code of honor, and are loyal only to their sisters. But when a siren does a truly cruel deed, she is banished to a desolate and dark place with water as black as night—a place where she'll never see her home or family again."

It clicked for Victoria. "They're banished here."

Fyrn nodded. "That's my best guess. No one quite likes the sirens, considering their habit of killing people, and thus we don't know much about them. Bornt's grandfather blocked off the tunnels leading to where we believe they are, and no one has been foolish enough to go there."

Victoria's eyes widened. "So the voices... The treasures..."

"Are the sirens showing travelers what they *want* to see rather than what is."

"But how do you know the Rhazdon Artifact is down there?" Audrey asked.

Everyone turned toward Fyrn, who frowned deeply. "Because I possess the only copy of the journal written by the explorer who hid it there."

"What?" Victoria and Audrey shouted in unison.

"When a Rhazdon Artifact is found, it must be hidden in a secure place where no one will steal it. Long ago, a well-meaning explorer was tasked by the Order of the Silver Griffins with disposing of a few. When he heard of the sirens below the city, he felt that would be a safe place to hide this one. Fairhaven became an unwitting host to dark magic."

"It's like winning a shitty lottery," Audrey said with a chuckle.

"Well, it's good luck for us," Victoria said. "We need that Rhazdon Artifact."

"What stops the sirens from using its magic?" Diesel asked.

Fyrn shrugged. "He was a wizard. All he said was that he charmed it, and no mortal could touch it."

"Great, more ominous and vague comments from wizards." Victoria rolled her eyes.

Audrey frowned. "But how do we get down there without being led to our deaths? That's what sirens do, right? Sing and kill people?"

Victoria chuckled. "Nice summary."

"We survive," Fyrn said sharply, looking at each of them, "by staying together. We walk with ropes tied to each other and cover our ears with enchanted cotton to block out their voices. Their magic only works if we can hear them. They will tempt you with your greatest desire and try to separate us, leading each of us to die through suffocation or starvation. They may even kill you themselves, if possible. They'll abandon you, and I can't urge this enough —if the cotton somehow gets removed, you absolutely must not listen to anything you hear down there, as sweet as their words may be. They're liars. It's all they know how to do, and if you do get caught in their web you must catch them in a lie to break free."

When he finished, no one spoke. Victoria stared at her feet, ruminating over Fyrn's warning.

They could all die down there.

"You shouldn't come," she said.

"Of course we're coming. You waited for me," Audrey said.

Victoria shook her head. "I was wrong. I didn't realize what was down there. Fyrn didn't tell me before now."

"Because I knew you would just leave, unprepared, on your own if I did," he muttered.

"Well, fine, then! You're right, I would have, and it's what I'm going to do now. I can't let you all go."

"I would never abandon you, my love," Diesel said, back stiffening. "I'm going."

Audrey pointed a thin finger at the wizard. "Yeah, what he said but without the clueless infatuation."

"Absolutely not," Victoria said, arms crossed.

Fyrn sighed impatiently. "Young woman, you are incredibly powerful. You killed a sphinx, freed Lochrose from thousands of years of imprisonment, and have by some miracle of nature not succumbed to the intense dark magic pumping through your blood. However, I have the only map in existence, and you will not—I want to stress this because it's important—you will *not* say no to us now."

Victoria's eyebrows rose nearly into her hair as she surveyed her three closest friends in the world: two wizards and an Atlantean. Audrey and Fyrn crossed their arms stubbornly, and Diesel set his hands on his hips. His eyes flitted briefly to the other two, and a second later he crossed his arms and frowned to match their expressions.

Despite her own stubborn pride, she couldn't help but feel grateful for the amazing people who would delve into the depths of Fairhaven for her. "Fine, you stubborn idiots."

"It's not quite thank you, but it'll do," Audrey said with a shrug.

Fyrn nodded once, apparently satisfied as well. "We're going deep into the earth, so we will need to perform some charms to protect us from the pressure changes. Nothing major, of course, but it would be enough to distract you from the task at hand. Hold still, the lot of you."

As the crystal at the tip of Fyrn's staff glowed with his magic, Victoria barely suppressed her smile. These three were stubborn and sometimes too pushy for their own good, but she loved them with all her heart.

CHAPTER SEVENTEEN

Led by the dim glow of the crystals atop Fyrn's and Diesel's staffs, Victoria followed her mentor and unrelenting admirer into the darkest tunnel she had ever seen in her life. The caves in Lochrose were a sunlit adventure compared to this. At least those caves had been covered in glimmering crystals. Down here there was only the darkness.

And the silence.

She scratched at the cotton in her ear, frustrated with the itchy substance. Beyond the dull thump of her heart and the slow rush of her breath, she couldn't hear a thing.

Now and then the rope connecting her to Audrey tugged as her friend lost her balance. Well, Victoria assumed that was it. Each time, she reached out and felt for Audrey's face. One time she accidentally poked an eye, and got a hearty slap on her hand.

Oops.

Fyrn led them down a side tunnel to the left she wouldn't have even seen on her own. The two glowing crystals were like wisps in a forest, and the surreal effect of being able to see nothing else began to grate on her nerves.

Just stick together, she told herself.

It would be okay if they just stuck together.

A finger ran along the back of Audrey's neck.

She jumped, cussing as she spun instinctively around. Though it was dark, she couldn't help wanting to look for whoever was touching her.

Or *what* was touching her.

The rope around her waist tightened as the party continued ahead of her, and she stumbled as Victoria's new inhuman strength pulling her along like she weighed nothing. Her body grazed the wall, and something yanked the cotton out of her ear.

Audrey slapped one hand firmly over her exposed ear and scanned the darkness, doing her best to reach for Victoria. She swung her arm frantically, and when she couldn't find her friend she turned her head in search of the glowing crystals that led their small party.

She saw only darkness.

"Audrey," a sweet voice said, echoing down the hall.

Master, please, the koi said in her mind. The voice was faded, as though he were trapped in a box.

Audrey shook her head. "Victoria! Where are you?"

"Audrey?" someone asked, the voice echoing down the hall.

Master, no! the koi said. So distant. So weak.

Victoria had been here mere seconds ago. Audrey just

had to catch up to her. She ran through the tunnel, breath heaving in her chest as she tried to keep one hand on her ear to block out anything the sirens said.

Then she tripped.

Audrey tumbled to the ground, the rock scraping her legs as she fell. Out of instinct, she reached out with both hands to catch herself.

"Audrey, come here!" a familiar voice shouted. It echoed, ethereal and unnerving.

Audrey ran.

Victoria followed the two crystals ahead of her, determined not to let them out of her sight. They gave her a sense of calmness, despite the fear building in her chest at being surrounded by the intense darkness.

She couldn't even see a foot behind her. It freaked her the hell out.

Behind her the rope tugged once again and she reached out, searching for Audrey's shoulder to help her stand.

Her hand met empty air.

Panicking, she reached again.

Nothing.

The rope loosened and she grabbed it, pulling on it as fast as she could, only to reach the end.

No Audrey.

"Guys, stop!" she shouted at the men ahead of her.

The two glowing crystals continued forward. With the enchanted cotton in their ears, neither of them could hear a thing.

She halted and spun on her heel, knowing full well that the rope would tighten and stop them. That was the point, after all.

Victoria retraced her steps, arms outstretched as she searched for Audrey's body. She couldn't be far.

The rope didn't tighten, and she looked again at the glowing crystals leading the way.

They were gone.

At most Victoria had turned her head for three seconds, and now she stood alone in the deepest caves beneath Fairhaven, surrounded by sirens who wanted to kill her and her friends.

To make it worse, they could be yelling for her and she wouldn't even know it. The enchanted cotton blocked out everything.

"I should have come alone," she said breathlessly.

***

"Audrey."

Audrey felt blindly through the darkness, following the sound of Victoria's voice. It had to be her, but the voice echoed. It seemed as though she were far down the hall, though Audrey couldn't understand how she'd gotten so far away.

The warm glow of a fire flickered to life in a nearby tunnel, casting an orange glow along the painfully dark walls. Audrey ran toward it, eager to find her friends, eager to be done with this, eager to be—

"Home?" she asked the empty air.

Though she had been in a dark tunnel seconds ago, she

now stood in her living room. The television flashed images from her favorite reality show, though the volume had been muted.

"No, this…this is…"

She had tried to say *wrong* but a sickly-sweet sensation combed through her brain. It was like the fuzzy fog that came with a migraine, too powerful and heavy to shake.

One hand on the back of her neck, she scanned the room again for clues. She had forgotten something.

Hadn't she?

The clink of dishes in the kitchen sink caught her attention, and she inched around the couch to get a view through the doorway. Two figures hovered over the stove, one with short blond hair and a stocky frame. The other chuckled and lifted a spoon with red sauce to her mouth, her long black hair almost identical to Audrey's.

"Mom? Dad?"

They spun, erupting into smiles as Audrey entered the kitchen. She walked toward them, her head fuzzy as she fought to remember how she had gotten here. A dull worry pressed in the back of her mind even as they pulled her into a hug.

She had forgotten something. Something big, but for the life of her she couldn't remember what it was.

The siren combed her thin fingers through Audrey's hair, her magic feeding her all the tidbits of information she needed to know—the girl's name, her fears, her greatest desires. In the middle of a small cave, Audrey stared blankly at the wall, fully lost in the hypnotic spell the siren had cast upon her.

With a warm and soothing hum, the siren spun her tale to her little victim. To her delicate and light-starved eyes, a dim blue glow illuminated the edges of everything in the cave. An underground river rushed nearby, eager to swallow anyone foolish enough to jump in. With every twist of her spell, she inched Audrey closer to the edge. It wouldn't be long now.

It wouldn't be long.

"You came for me, Fyrn," a sweet voice said in his ear.

"Maria?" His heart broke at the sound of her voice, a voice he hadn't heard in decades.

He strode through a dim cave, the one he had lost her in so long ago. The tunnel to the beast, a failed promise to protect her from its hunger.

The greatest mistake he had ever made, and now he could set it right.

But he couldn't recall how he had arrived. He simply knew with all his heart that she was here. *Finally* he had figured out how to find her, and his nerves hummed with anticipation at seeing her once more. The sickening haze of a headache clawed at the back of his mind, but he fought to keep it at bay.

"I knew you loved me," she said, her voice echoing through the tunnel.

"Forever," he said softly. He limped forward, desperate to find her again.

Diesel pressed his back against the cold, rocky wall with one hand covering his left ear to block out any siren song. Keeping his staff tucked in the crook of one arm, his eyes scanned the darkness. He waited for the creature hiding in its shadows to swipe at him again. It had grabbed one of the cotton swabs from his ears, but this time he was ready for it.

Fingers crept up his neck, cool and soft ,and he inched his hand closer, letting it think it had him until it was close enough to grab. The creature moved painfully slowly, almost leisurely in its pace until its hand had reached his right ear.

When he knew he wouldn't fail, he pounced.

The figure before him gasped, and he triumphantly lit the light at the tip of his staff.

Victoria stood in his arms, eyes wide.

He hesitated. He had covered his ear the moment the swab had been pulled out, so he didn't think this could be siren magic. Of course, there was the risk that when the swab had come out he had succumbed.

Victoria said something, her voice muffled by the cotton in one ear and his hand covering the other, and he gritted his teeth in frustration. If this was her he needed to hear what she said—but this could all be a ploy.

Of course, if he had already succumbed to the siren song, covering his ear wouldn't do any good.

Gingerly, he lifted his hand only a little. "What?"

"I lost the others," Victoria said, breathless. "I'm so

grateful I found you, Diesel. I'm so scared. What do we do?"

She leaned her head against his chest, and his heart involuntarily skipped a beat at her touch. He relaxed slightly, grateful she trusted him so completely. "I'll get us out of this, Victoria. I'll—"

His gaze drifted down to the woman holding him, the woman he wanted more than anything in this world. She wrapped her arms around him tightly, body trembling slightly as she asked him to save her.

This was what he wanted—to save the woman he loved —but Victoria would never cower like this. She didn't tremble. It was an insult to her strength, and the sirens had taken his wish too far.

He grabbed her neck and pinned her against the wall. The woman struggled, gasping for air. "Diesel, my darling! You're hurting me!"

"You are a liar, siren," he snapped.

The fearful, panicked expression on Victoria's face bled away in an instant to a smug smirk. "That I am, darling. That I am."

The siren vanished beneath him, and he scrambled to find the second piece of cotton to protect his ears.

He had to find the real Victoria before he lost her forever.

Victoria sucker-punched yet another face in the darkness.

For the last ten minutes invisible hands had crept along her body, all of them reaching for the cotton in her ears.

Her strength alone had kept them at bay, but in her frustration she had taken up swinging wildly into the darkness.

Not the best attack strategy, but so far it was working.

Victoria.

She snapped her head up at the voice, panicking. Her hands shot to her ears in the fear that the sirens had pulled out the cotton, but both pieces were there. She scanned the darkness, desperate to know where the voice had come from.

Victoria, damn it, turn around.

She spun to find Shiloh in the middle of the tunnel, his body illuminated by a dull white glow. He pointed to the pitch-black wall.

What are you doing? she asked.

Leading you to the Rhazdon Artifact. I can feel it. It's close.

Victoria hesitated as another pair of hands wound around her waist. She grabbed one and bent the fingers back until she felt a satisfying crack. The hand twisted in her grip until she let it go, and it disappeared into the darkness. If she didn't still have the cotton in her ears, she imagined she would have heard a sharp wail of pain.

Good. That'd teach the shadow monsters to feel her up.

Shiloh impatiently pointed to the tunnel again, rolling his eyes. *I'm not a hallucination. Your cotton balls are firmly seated in that dense head of yours.*

Ah, there we go. An insult, so it was definitely the real Shiloh.

She jogged behind him as he led her through the tunnels. The hands continued to touch her, and with each step they became more forceful. They sometimes pulled on her shirt and other times tried to trip her.

They didn't want her going this way.

She smirked, running faster as Shiloh sped through the tunnels. *Almost there.*

Elle appeared beside him, laughing and clapping her hands. *Oh, are we racing? First one to that set of doors up there wins!*

You are absolutely useless, Elle, he muttered.

Wait, what doors? Victoria asked. She squinted, trying to make out anything more than the sheer blackness of the dark tunnels but could only see Shiloh's form a few feet ahead of her.

With a sudden rush he disappeared, and a second later Victoria slammed her head against something hard. The force knocked her on her ass and she groaned in surprise.

Two brilliant metal doors swung open from the force, and light streamed from somewhere overhead. A single pedestal sat in the middle of the room.

This was it…had to be.

She jumped to her feet and rushed inside. There was a golden amulet on the pedestal, and a dull green glow emanated from its center like an iris in an eye.

She shuddered.

The sensation of being watched crept over her skin, and she looked over her shoulder expecting to finally see the bodies those hands belonged to. Instead, she saw the open doors and inky darkness hovering just outside. It was as though the doorway were a portal to space itself, and taking one step beyond would mean being lost.

For whatever reason, the creatures that had tried to keep her at bay wouldn't walk into the room's light. They huddled outside, perhaps waiting for her to leave.

"You can't stop me," she said to the shadows.

As if on cue, a dozen hands shot from the darkness in the hallway. They grabbed her arms, and she kicked them back as forcefully as she could. Unseen assailants started to pull her back into the hallway, the sheer number of them almost overwhelming her.

But she was so close.

With her right hand, she grabbed the amulet off the pedestal, and when she touched it her skin blistered as though burned by fire. She grimaced, wondering if the wizard who hid it here had charmed it to burn whoever touched it.

Didn't matter.

As the amulet burned her, the magic tied to the dagger embedded in her arm healed her. For each second of pain, she was given a second of relief.

The wizard's charm couldn't stop her.

With her left hand, Victoria summoned her sword and hacked through the pale gray hands reaching for her. Each slice produced black blood, and she could imagine the screams.

Thank goodness the cotton blocked them out.

"Enough!" Victoria shouted. She stabbed the shadows beyond the door, driving her blade as deep as it would go. The hands stopped and fell limp, disappearing one by one into the intense darkness beyond the small room.

As the world around her stilled, Victoria heaved. Riddled with nerves, she waited for something to happen, for another hand to reach out and try to grab her.

Instead, pain ripped up her right arm and clear into her teeth. She screamed in agony and fell to her knees, and the world swirled around her as the familiar agony reminded her how much she *hated* fusing with Rhazdon Artifacts.

Apparently she had in fact killed at least one of the creatures that had attacked her.

She held on, trying to stay awake through the pain in case any of the monsters had survived.

But she couldn't.

Her sword disappeared as her vision went dark, and before long she collapsed onto the ground.

CHAPTER EIGHTEEN

Victoria woke to a very angry pair of eyes glaring down at her.

She yelped in surprise and threw a punch at the strange woman, only to have her hand sail through the delicate nose.

A ghost.

Victoria sat on her heels, tense and nervous as she sized up the woman glowering down at her. A rich white cape covered her shoulders, and its fur lining swept the floor. The stranger lifted an elegant chin and her mouth moved, although Victoria couldn't hear her through the cotton still in her ears.

"What?"

The regal woman rolled her eyes. *You woke me up. Why?*

"Sorry," Victoria said, standing. "I need the Rhazdon Artifact you're tied to."

Nonsense! Your needs don't matter. Let me sleep once more.

Victoria chuckled. "Fine. Go to sleep."

The woman gestured to Victoria's hand. *Take it off and return it to the platform.*

"Removing the Artifact would kill me."

And?

Victoria laughed, shaking her head. "As charming as you are, I have things to do. Go away."

Ridiculous! I won't let you—

"Enough." Victoria snapped her fingers, focusing the full force of her bear artifact's power into dismissing the horrible woman from her presence. The ghost disappeared, leaving only the silent room in her wake.

Victoria peeked into the hallway, where the oppressive darkness had lifted. On the ground was a dark pool of what could only be blood, and streaks indicating that someone had dragged a body down the tunnel.

"Why didn't they kill me while I was unconscious?" she asked the empty room.

They seemed terrified of the light, Shiloh said.

Victoria peeked through her hair at Shiloh, who was leaning against the nearby wall. He sighed deeply as though he weren't talking about sirens nearly murdering her.

We waved and hollered, too! Elle said, skipping through the tunnel just outside.

Victoria smiled and her shoulders relaxed. "You saved me, didn't you?"

Shiloh shrugged. *I didn't want to be trapped down here with those two.*

"Thanks, Shiloh."

Her right hand ached, and Victoria lifted it to find the golden amulet embedded in her palm. She gulped, stunned at the green glow radiating from what used to be skin. It lit the air around her like a beacon, the grim eye of the amulet forever a part of her now.

And its powers were hers as well.

In the silence of the deep tunnel, Victoria did her best to come up with a plan. Yes, she had found the Rhazdon Artifact, but at what cost?

Audrey, Fyrn, and Diesel were roaming the tunnels at this very moment, lost and probably alone.

Well, not alone. They likely had sirens to keep them company.

Victoria bristled, gritting her teeth. "Shiloh. Elle."

What do you want now, woman? Shiloh snapped from behind her.

Good old Shiloh.

Without turning around, Victoria pointed into the tunnel. "Can you find my friends?"

Elle's giggle echoed in Victoria's mind. *Oh, a searching game?*

Shiloh rolled his eyes. *Victoria, we found the Rhazdon Artifact because we have similar magic. We can't go on quests for you willy-nilly.*

She frowned. "Then how—"

Victoria stared at the glowing green amulet fused with her hand. Fyrn didn't know much about its powers, but he had told her it bestowed divination magic. She could read possible outcomes.

But how?

She glanced at the illuminated room and its empty pedestal. If she stayed here much longer—

Fast as lightning, an image flashed in her mind of her

corpse leaning against the pedestal, an arm clutched her stomach as if it ached for food.

Starvation.

The word rang in her head like thunder, and she snapped out of the vision as quickly as she could.

"Oh, this power is going to be *super*-fun," she snapped, disgusted with the image she had been forced to endure.

She would have to be more careful of any what-if scenarios she asked herself.

Taking a deep breath, she stared into the darkness beyond the open doors, where the light streaming from this room illuminated three pathways. She turned toward the first one, hoping one of these tunnels would take her to her friends.

"Here goes," she muttered to herself.

"How I've missed you, my darling," Maria's sweet voice in his ear warmed Fyrn to the core. Her soft arms wound around his neck as she sat behind him, petting his hair.

"I missed you as well." He leaned into her, happy for the first time in decades despite the buzzing haze clouding his mind.

"You will stay with me, won't you?"

"Of course."

"Forever?"

"Forever."

"Good, my love. Good."

"Fyrn, snap out of it!" someone yelled.

He shot upright, glancing around the empty tunnel.

Blue light streamed in from holes in the rock overhead. The voice had been familiar, but he couldn't place why.

The soft hands on his shoulders yanked him backward, and he was once more in Maria's arms. "The beast is back, my dear! You must—"

"Fyrn!"

Someone slapped him hard across the face. In a split second the blue light faded to almost utter darkness, and the soft hand on his shoulder was now cold and clammy. He struggled to stand, but it held him in place.

A vague silhouette stood over him and knelt, driving a sword into the air by his head. The slick squelch of a sword through flesh rocked him to his core.

Confused and panicking, he grabbed his staff and lit the gem on its tip. He had to find Maria, had to rescue her. He couldn't lose her again, not—

The light from his staff illuminated the world around him and Victoria came into view. She knelt at his side, her eyes wide as she stared at him. "Are you okay?"

The hands on his shoulders loosened and a body fell to the ground.

"Maria!" he screamed.

He tilted his staff until the light revealed a pale gray corpse. Silver hair covered her face, and a pool of black blood grew beneath her body.

Understanding crashed into Fyrn like a tsunami. Maria was dead—she had been for decades. He would never have her back. Somehow the sirens had tricked him into removing the cotton.

They had toyed with him, and Victoria had saved his life.

Despite the grieving he had done to clear Maria from his life, a deep sense of loss tightened his throat. He shook his head, trying to focus on the moment, but it was several seconds before he could once more swallow the pain.

"Fyrn?" Victoria asked softly.

"We have to find the others," he said, not wanting to answer the many questions that were probably buzzing through her mind.

He hadn't spoken about Maria to anyone, and he didn't plan to start now—not even Victoria.

It took nearly two hours, but she finally found the others and led them out of the tunnels holding hands, with fresh enchanted cotton from her pack in every ear.

No one would tell her what the sirens had tempted them away with. She found Diesel sobbing over a rock in the middle of the tunnel, and Audrey had been about to go for a swim in the most dangerous rapids Victoria had ever seen in her life.

The sirens had toyed with their brains, and no one wanted to discuss what they had seen. She couldn't blame them.

As they walked, Victoria desperately wished to yank the scratchy cotton out of her ears. The fibers had tickled her eardrum for hours. They were almost out of siren territory though, and she wouldn't pull the cotton out until she was sure it was safe.

As the oppressive darkness in the tunnels slowly faded Fyrn gestured for them to pull out the cotton, and Victoria did so with a deep breath of gratitude. "Ugh, that was like having a Q-tip rammed into my head for hours on end."

"Victoria," Fyrn said, voice stern.

Ugh. That was his boring lecture voice.

"Yes?"

"From the bottom of my heart, I thank you. I will never tell you what I experienced or who—" his voice broke, and his hard eyes softened, "or who the siren pretended to be, but I am grateful nonetheless for what you did."

Victoria's shoulders relaxed. She had expected a lecture, not gratitude. "You're welcome."

Diesel leaned on his staff, staring at the ground. "I saw you dead, Victoria. When the sirens couldn't fool me, they forced me to watch horrible things. I couldn't escape it. They put on a performance of every death I've ever feared you would meet."

Victoria's mouth dropped open. She didn't know what to say, but now his sobbing over a rock suddenly made far more sense.

"They showed me home," Audrey said softly. "They showed me Mom and Dad. With everything going on, I didn't realize how much I missed them."

Victoria just swallowed hard.

"Did you succeed?" Fyrn asked, looking right at her.

With a sigh, Victoria lifted her hand and stretched out her palm for them to see. Audrey and Diesel gasped as the glowing golden eye winked back at them, shimmering and stunning, a work of art forever fused with her skin.

"Then it was worth the agony," Fyrn said softly.

"Fyrn—"

"No, Victoria. I'm fine, so give us an update. What do you know of your powers? The ghost?"

Victoria rubbed her wrist, still not used to the constant tension in her palm from the newest Artifact. "It burned me pretty badly when I picked it up. I guess that's the charm the wizard who put it there used. He wanted it to kill whoever found it."

"Probably."

"The ghost is this rude but regal woman. She looked like a queen."

Fyrn nodded. "That corroborates what I've learned so far. If my research is correct, she was a witch queen around the time Rhazdon was amassing his armies."

"Well, she's also a bitch."

Fyrn chuckled. "Yes, that sounds about right."

"I can keep her at bay, although any time I don't focus my will on keeping her out of sight she pops up."

"Recruit your other ghosts to help you. They may be able to keep her in check. And remember, Victoria—she will try to kill you. She has killed other hosts in the past."

Victoria groaned. *Super*-fun.

Audrey chuckled. "You glow like a jack-o-lantern. Can you turn it off?"

Victoria laughed. "I don't think so."

"Well, if we ever need a searchlight we'll come looking for you, Rudolph."

Audrey and Diesel laughed, holding their sides while Victoria rolled her eyes and did her best to suppress a broad grin. "You're all idiots."

She stared at the Artifact, her smile faltering slightly as it glimmered. This wasn't something she could hide, maybe not even with gloves if the glow was bright enough. Bit by bit, the Artifacts had made themselves a part of her in a way she couldn't hide anymore.

And you know what? I don't want to hide.

"What about your powers?" Diesel lifted her hand in his, running his finger along the golden rim of the magical item in her hand. It was more of a curious gesture than an intimate one, but his warm touch sent a spark through her arm.

"I used the divination ability to find you three. I don't know the other two powers."

"How does it work?" Fyrn asked.

"I ask a what-if question, and I get a vision with the possible outcome."

Diesel's eyes lit up. "Really? What if I grew a beard?"

Out of impulse more than curiosity, Victoria briefly considered what he might look like. In an instant, a crystal-clear vision of a lopsided goatee flashed in her mind.

She shuddered. "Don't."

"Fascinating," Fyrn said under his breath.

Victoria stretched out her hand. "Is this enough, Fyrn? Am I finally ready?"

He smiled, the first since they'd left the siren's lair. "You are, Victoria. You most certainly are."

CHAPTER NINETEEN

It was close to three in the morning when their small party returned to the refugee camp, and Victoria could barely keep her eyes open. After the rush of adrenaline had faded, the long trek back had taken its toll on her.

Only sheer force of will had kept her moving.

Their return trip had taken several days. They had opted against using a portal, since that meant calling on complex magic when both their wizards were emotionally exhausted. After all, Diesel had watched her die at least a dozen different ways, and Fyrn—well, his trauma had been one Victoria was quite certain he would never share.

After climbing seven flights of stairs, Victoria sank into her borrowed bed. The ogres had carved cliff dwellings into the walls to make more room for the refugees as they arrived, and the elves had used their magic to refine the spaces into comfortable living quarters. Thus far it was her favorite bedroom, perhaps second only to the mansion she had shared with Audrey after realizing she was loaded.

Styx was already snoozing on her pillow. As she

stretched out on the mattress, the little pixie nestled up to her in his sleep. She smiled and shut her eyes, promising herself she would bathe in the morning. If she did it now, she would probably fall asleep in the tub.

Victoria woke to several trumpets sounding outside. Styx was gone.

She scrambled out of bed and got caught in the blankets, landing with a hard thud on the floor. It took several moments of cursing under her breath to wrench free and leap toward the window.

An army marched in the wide road below. Ten men across, shoulder to shoulder, farther than Victoria could see through the open hole that served as her window.

In her exhausted state, she panicked. Luak had found them. He had brought an army, and—

At the head of the troops, a familiar feminine figure lifted a thin hand. The troops behind her stopped as she scanned the refugee camp.

Angelique.

Still dressed in her travel clothes from the day before, Victoria raced down the steps to give her friend a piece of her mind. After several minutes of running Victoria finally made it to the street.

"Ah, there you are!" Angelique shouted to her from her position at the head of the troops. General Eldrin stood beside her and stopped speaking as Victoria neared.

As Victoria passed them, several of the Lochrose soldiers smiled or nudged their neighbors. Perhaps they recognized her, but she had met so many people in Lochrose that she could hardly remember them all.

When she reached the queen, Victoria rubbed her eyes and yawned. "What are you doing, blaring your horn like that?"

Angelique laughed. "That's not quite the welcome I was expecting, but I suppose it's the one I *should* have expected from you. It's a pleasure to see you as well, Victoria."

"I truly am grateful to see you, Angelique, and even sooner than expected. But come on, why did you need to blast us all awake with horns? Was that necessary? Needed to wake everyone up to say hi?"

Angelique swept a lock of hair out of Victoria's face, not even bothering to hide her smirk. "Victoria, it's noon. I'm fairly certain you were the only one asleep."

"I… Um, I knew that."

"Of course you…" Angelique's eyes drifted to Victoria's right hand, and her words died in her throat.

Victoria nervously squeezed her right hand closed, but she couldn't hide the brilliant green glow.

"So that's where you all went," Eldrin said softly.

Victoria eyed the newly-promoted general, wondering what the elf would do. "Are you upset?"

He chewed the interior of his cheek for a moment as if considering the question. "If it were anyone else, I would kill them for this blatant act of treason."

"But you, Victoria Brie, are different," Angelique finished for him.

Victoria smiled. "In that case, let's get your soldiers settled in."

"And you back in bed," Eldrin added with a cursory glance at her hair.

Victoria swept a hand through her tangled locks. "Yeah, that sounds amazing."

Eight more hours of sleep and a hot meal later, Victoria lounged on one of the tattered couches in the sitting area the officials and politicians shared in their little cave dwelling.

"I really *am* glad to see you, Angelique," she said.

The Lochrose queen leaned against the wall next to the smokeless fire, smiling as she watched Victoria. "It's great to see you, too, even if that was a terrible welcome."

Victoria laughed. "You interrupted the first real sleep I'd had in about a week. Sorry if I was grouchy."

"Sirens, huh?" Angelique rubbed her head, still marveling at the tale Fyrn had shared with the assembled leaders in the war room while Victoria had slept.

To Victoria's surprise, no one had been upset. At least that was what Fyrn had told her, although he wasn't the best at reading emotions. Judging by the lack of death threats, though, it seemed as though the people of the Fairhaven resistance didn't care if she had twelve Rhazdon Artifacts so long as she killed Luak.

"Worth it," Victoria said absently as she stared at the glowing green amulet in her palm.

"What does it do?"

Victoria grinned. "Oh, so we're sharing state secrets now?"

Angelique laughed. "Your powers are a state secret?"

"Oh, yes. Very sensitive data. Top secret, I'm afraid."

The queen shook her head ruefully. "You're an idiot."

"I'm adorable."

"So, come on… What can you do? What's worth facing certain death at the hands of sirens?"

Victoria sighed and stretched out on the couch, draping her arms over her head. In her mind, she debated what would happen if she told Angelique the truth. This was a powerful monarch, after all, and one she didn't know too well yet.

A vision flashed in her mind of Angelique grimacing a mere minute in the future, not quite certain Victoria was telling the truth about her powers. She would ask what would happen if they walked outside right now, and when they walked outside, her general would suggest she duel with Victoria to entertain the troops and help them burn off some nervous energy by reminding them of the sheer power on their side of the war.

Several more visions flashed in her mind of the nine times Angelique would ask for help, knowing full well that Victoria would decide whether the course of action would be prudent. Famine. Pending war. Would a charming young suitor make a good king? The requests would be few and far between, always spoken with respect, and never abused.

Safe. The word echoed in her mind.

Good enough.

"Divination. That's all I know so far."

"Divination?"

"I can tell what will happen, although it has limits. I

have to ask outright, pose a what-if question to myself, but it seems to work rather well."

"What happens if—"

"When we walk outside, your general will ask us to duel so we can entertain the troops and help them burn off nervous energy."

Angelique's jaw dropped open, and Victoria couldn't help the cocky smirk that spread across her face.

"Gods," the queen muttered.

Victoria stood and opened the door. "Want to test my theory?"

Without a word, Angelique stepped into the hallway and led the way outside. Every now and then she glanced nervously at Victoria, who just chuckled silently to herself. She would have to be more careful about displaying this power, since apparently it really freaked people out.

As soon as they stepped outside, Angelique's general ran over, huffing. "There you are, my queen! I came to ask if—"

"Yes, General, I will spar with the host," she interrupted.

A look of utter shock spread across his face, and that seemed to be all the proof Angelique needed. He stuttered, but eventually he led them into the street to meet the gathered fighters.

As they walked, Angelique leaned in close to whisper. "You're right, Victoria, that was definitely worth every step in the siren's domain."

Victoria grinned. It certainly was.

CHAPTER TWENTY

At the evening banquet, Victoria had a *tad* too much to drink.

It was hardly her fault, of course. The elvish waiters filling the goblets at her table simply never let a cup sit empty.

And, come on… She couldn't waste *wine*.

Angelique sat to her right, and Audrey to her left. The meal had gone on for a good hour before the diners had left one by one for bed or to dance in the street. A band had assembled by the road, plucking guitars and harps while the men sang cheery songs. Couples twirled around each other on the rocky ground, everyone laughing as they spun.

Still lounging at the table, Victoria's companions leaned in occasionally, full of mischief and laughter amidst the music. The plates were long gone, but they all seemed rather interested in when the server was coming around with more drinks.

After all, a war was on the horizon—they had little time left to enjoy themselves before the battle.

Angelique summoned the server with an elegant wave of her wrist. Her speech slurred only slightly, and Victoria was quite certain no one else would notice the subtle droop of her eyelids.

The young elf bowed as he approached the queen. "Yes, Your Majesty?"

"See that those guarding the exits and scouting get a full plate of food and several glasses of wine when they come back."

"Of course, Your Majesty."

"Very good." She nodded, but the dip of her head was a little too slow.

Victoria giggled and leaned in. "You're drunk. You're a regal drunk, but you are drunk nonetheless."

"A queen is never drunk, Miss Victoria," Angelique said with a mischievous twist to her lips. "She merely talks slower and takes greater care to enunciate her words."

Laughter bubbled out of Victoria's chest, and she nearly snorted at the sheer ridiculousness of watching a drunk witch try to explain her way out of being caught.

"Oh, oh!" Angelique gestured for Victoria and Audrey to lean in. "I almost forgot. I have a present for the both of you. Come with me."

"A present!" Audrey giggled.

"A present. Come!" The witch ushered them up a staircase.

Despite the drunken fog from the wine, suspicion flared in the back of Victoria's mind. She asked her new magic if this was safe—an overly simplistic question, but all her fuzzy mind could muster—and the answer came back loud and clear.

Safe.

Good enough.

Victoria and Audrey followed Angelique as she led them through a series of corridors and exits. A few times they passed a wizard guard she had posted, each of whom chuckled and nodded in greeting as the women passed.

Finally Angelique stopped at a large wooden door. Its ancient golden hinges were covered in grime, but the queen waited breathlessly for Victoria. "Are you ready?"

"What is this?" Victoria asked, sobering a bit from the long walk.

"My soldiers found this while scouting for alternate routes for the coming war. It won't work for an attack, but it is rather lovely. See for yourselves." She pushed open the door, which swung on silent hinges.

Pale blue moonlight glowed as Victoria stepped out onto a walkway high above Fairhaven. Below her, the city slept in deceptive peace. The massive cavern looked even larger from up here, and the crystal ceiling dominated the view. It was only a hundred feet or so above her, the stunning light reminding her of all she loved in this fair city.

Far below, the towering white castle reached toward the longest crystal, its tallest spire nearly touching the crystal's tip.

Angelique sat on a nearby boulder, kicking her legs as she sighed happily. "Growing up, I never believed I would see another kingdom. I always dreamed of traveling to every great kemana, seeing them for myself, but I never believed it could happen—not to me."

Victoria put her arm around the queen's shoulders and pulled her in for a hug. "I'm glad Fairhaven was your first stop, though I wish it had been under different circumstances."

"Me, too," the queen said.

"You gave me a new life, Victoria. You gave all of my people a new life, and we are forever in your debt."

Audrey hiccupped and leaned against a nearby wall. "Hey, I helped!"

The queen chuckled. "That you did, Audrey. I'm sorry. Thank you both."

"She always gets the credit," Audrey said with a wink toward Victoria.

Victoria laughed it off and looked at her beautiful city. Fairhaven twinkled back at her, a few lights in a few windows reminding her that it was not empty. It was not dead. It sought freedom, and freedom was on the horizon.

"This was a perfect present, Angelique. Thank you."

"I have one more," Angelique said with a devious smile.

"Oh?"

The queen whipped out a flask from her robe. "A queen always comes prepared. Shall we continue?"

Victoria laughed. "I knew I liked you."

Thanks to her healing ability, Victoria didn't have much of a hangover the next day. Angelique and Audrey, however, were nowhere to be found.

In fact, most of the refugee camp seemed to be recovering. Only a few sober individuals were around to serve breakfast, so Victoria took what was available and offered her thanks before heading to the war room.

She might as well brainstorm.

With a piece of bread in one hand, she circled the map of Fairhaven while Styx hummed happily to himself on her shoulder and stuffed crumbs into his tiny face. Looking out over the city last night had ignited a fire in her to iron out the details of their attack as soon as possible. Every second she waited, Luak grew stronger.

Little figurines littered the map, each representing a dozen warriors. They had a fair number of wizards and witches, with quite a few ogres and not nearly enough elves to balance out the army.

The bread crunched in her mouth as she absently

chewed, debating her options. If she moved them to the banking sector, perhaps the tall buildings could serve as cover and funnel Luak's troops into the main road. Or perhaps she could send the ogre platoons down Main Street to retake the town square.

She frowned. No, no, no. Everything she did put too many lives at risk.

With a frustrated flick of her wrist, she brushed a few bread crumbs off the map and leaned against the table. If only they had the golems—they were the missing piece. Yes, her divination helped, as would the other two powers in her newest Rhazdon Artifact—if she knew what they were—but these golems would save many lives if they could take the brunt of the attack.

In her musing, her attention to keeping her newest ghost at bay slipped.

The beautiful woman appeared on the other side of the table, fanning herself in disgust. "How dare you coop me up and deny me my right to walk around! Why, if you only—"

Victoria groaned in annoyance. "Now I see how you led those other Rhazdon hosts to their deaths. You must have talked until they jumped off a bridge to make it stop."

The woman scowled. "I'll have you know in my day I was a woman of power and prestige. I would have had you killed simply for your dismissive tone."

Victoria chuckled. "You remind me of someone I read about in a book once."

The ghost leaned back slightly, a look of mild curiosity creeping into the constant scowl. "Who? Someone important?"

"The Queen of Hearts from *Alice in Wonderland*. She was loud and crude too."

The ghost stomped her foot, mouth agape in apparent offence. "How dare you! I will not be spoken to this way. I am a witch of notoriety and profound ability! No one—"

In the back of Victoria's mind something clicked into place. She tuned out whatever nonsense the ghost queen was spouting and raised a hand to stop her. "What did you say?"

The ghost frowned. "You don't even listen. I'm a powerful witch, you insolent fool, and you will not treat me—"

"Something profound," Victoria said softly. A wild grin spread across her lips as the pieces clicked into place. "Only a connection to something profound can direct their rage."

"Oh, lovely, now she's prattling nonsense," the ghost muttered.

"Fyrn!" Victoria shouted, ignoring the queen as she ran out of the war room. "I have an idea!"

It took a while to locate Fyrn, but she eventually found him buried beneath the blankets in his bed. He groaned and turned over any time she tried to get him to listen to her newest idea, waving her away each time.

She chuckled. "Fyrn, are you hungover?"

A single weathered hand appeared from beneath the blankets and pointed to the door.

"This is important!"

"Victoria, damn it," he muttered through the blankets. His finger pointed again to the door.

"You're a wizard. Just heal the hangover so we can get on with this."

"I was sleeping until you barged in, young woman," he snapped through the blankets.

"Well, just listen! The golems need to connect with something profoundly powerful, right? So we fuse them with a Rhazdon Artifact! Those are objects of intensely powerful magic. Then whoever controls the Artifact controls the golems. Problem solved!"

He sat upright in bed, the blankets covering everything but his head. His long white beard poofed out around him, giving him the overall appearance of a head shoved through very old cotton candy.

Victoria bit back a chuckle.

"Well, you're the one who barged in unannounced, so you need to deal with the unpleasant view," he muttered. Nonetheless, he stroked his poofy beard with a thoughtful gleam in his eye. "Your plan could work."

"I knew it!"

"But it's risky. Whatever we fuse them with will be permanent. I don't believe we can change it, so if the object falls in the wrong hands, they'll not only be a Rhazdon host but also have control over a powerful army."

"Let's make sure it doesn't fall in the wrong hands, then."

He frowned. "I can't guarantee this will work. Yes, the new Rhazdon Artifact is intensely more powerful than the others, but I can't be certain…"

"Is there any way to be certain?"

Fyrn blew a raspberry. "Turning them on."

"So basically this is either going to work or destroy everything?"

"Pretty much, yes."

She sighed and leaned against the wall, running through her options. "Your golems are deep in the tunnels on the opposite side of Fairhaven. If we turn them on and this fails we could lock them in there, right? You charmed that cave?"

Fyrn groaned. "Yes, but these represent decades of research and implementation, not to mention the most powerful relic in existence."

"So you're afraid of losing your science project?"

Fyrn scowled, glaring at her with the full force of a grumpy old man who had just been woken up by an unwanted visitor.

"Well? Is Fairhaven worth the risk?" she prodded.

His gaze softened. "Yes, it is."

She clapped her hands together, victorious. "Let's get to work, then."

CHAPTER TWENTY-TWO

Truth be told, Victoria was having second thoughts. She had forgotten how damn big these golems were. Styx hid in her hair, his tiny eyes peeking through her locks as he shivered.

The thirty golems towered around her in Fyrn's enchanted cavern, easily twenty feet tall while seated. They were arranged side by side along the walls of the massive cavern, curled into balls as they slept.

Soon they would wake up and either bow to her will or try with all their might to rip her and Fyrn apart.

She gulped.

"Victoria," Fyrn said with a nod to the brilliant crystal sitting on the pedestal before him. It sparked and glowed with vibrant blue light.

"Here goes," she muttered.

Fyrn consulted the book he held in one hand and grasped his staff with the other. "Whatever the object, you must place it and it alone in the crystal."

"In? It looks pretty solid to me."

"Looks can be deceiving."

"Thanks, Cryptic Wizard Stereotype."

He frowned. "Just put the amulet on the crystal, and be careful not to let your hand go inside. That might connect *you* to the golems instead of the Rhazdon Artifact."

"Which would still work, right?"

"Until you die, probably, then the golems would be without a master. So focus, girl. Are you ready?"

"As I'll ever be," she said under her breath.

Victoria set her right palm on the crystal, which sparked and sputtered at her touch. The brilliant light within the crystal spun, twirling as if there were a tornado within its depths.

A powerful tug on her artifact yanked her closer to the crystal and she yelled in surprise, despising the sensation. If even one of her Rhazdon Artifacts was pulled out, she would die.

The crystal tugged again.

Around her, the cavern shook. The golems stirred to life, rocks and pebbles falling to the ground as they lifted their heads. Their eyes glowed with the same brilliant blue as the relic powering them, and one by one they turned their massive heads to her.

She gritted her teeth as the crystal tugged once again on her Artifact. "Fyrn, you can do your thing any day now."

"The spell has been cast, Victoria. All we can do is wait." He snapped the book shut and stowed it in his robe. With a nervous glance around at the golems, he gripped his staff a bit tighter.

With a final tug, the crystal pulled on her Rhazdon Artifact so sharply that her hand slipped inside. Her arm simply disappeared at the wrist and she did her best to pull it out, but the pull was too strong, the relic's magic too powerful.

Fyrn cursed loudly. "Victoria, what did I *just say* about your hand?"

"Working on it, thanks for your concern!"

The golems stood, their deafening roars shaking rocks from the cave's ceiling. Fyrn blasted several of them to pebbles before they could hit Victoria, but the monsters began to close in.

"Victoria, pull your hand out now!"

She tugged with all her might, her enhanced grip on the pedestal crushing the rock to dust. "I can't!"

"Victoria, you have to get your hand out of there!"

"I-I..." She gritted her teeth as the golems closed in, several of the nearest ones reaching for her.

"Victoria!"

"STOP!" she screamed, her voice booming with an ethereal quality she didn't recognize.

The golems obeyed, freezing in place. The tension on her hand lessened as the crystal released her, and she yanked her arm free with one final desperate tug.

Heart thudding in her chest, she glanced at the golems. Their eyes had faded from the blue of the crystal to a familiar green, and she glanced down at her hand to see her amulet glowing with all the fire of the relic it had been submerged in. Thankfully her skin didn't glow at all.

"I think it worked," she said.

Fyrn didn't answer, just shot her a barely-veiled look of panic mixed with relief.

Yeah, that had definitely been too close for comfort, but they'd gotten what they had come for.

Now…on to Victory!

CHAPTER TWENTY-THREE

Audrey bit into an apple as she lounged against the wall in the war room. Several of the politicians grimaced in disgust, but she wouldn't stop eating her favorite fruit just because the people of Fairhaven thought it was nothing more than feed for cattle.

Besides, she loved the way it irked them.

The curtain lifted as Victoria entered, followed by Fyrn, the final two to join the discussions about the battle that would make or break Fairhaven.

No pressure.

"Ah, there you are," Eldrin said as the host entered. He brushed off his hands and leaned against the table holding their map.

"We don't have much time," Lady Spry said from beside the fire, her arms folded across her chest. She stood as still as a statue, and Audrey could almost see her tremble with anticipation.

Victoria nodded to the senator. "Lady Spry, an update please."

"He's horrible," the elegant woman muttered, her gaze falling to the ground.

Everyone waited in silence, and even Audrey stopped munching on her apple. Lady Spry wasn't one for outbursts or saying anything that deviated from the task at hand, but she lifted a thin hand to her face to wipe away a tear. In the firelight her fingers shook.

Diesel put an arm around the witch, and that seemed to snap her out of it. She nodded once in gratitude and stepped out of his reach. "Since his fight with Victoria, Luak has begun to murder the people of the castle in their beds, demanding their magical artifacts and charms. He has forced the witches and wizards left in the city to cast charms and spells day and night to shield the castle and to protect him. We're including failsafes where we can, but he has already killed so many of us."

Every head hung in remorse as her words settled on the room, and for a moment, no one spoke.

Victoria finally broke the spell by tapping on the map. "We will win."

Lady Spry nodded. "You'd damn well better."

"We have new allies," Victoria added, with a glance over her shoulder at Fyrn.

Eldrin perked up, the points of his elvish ears twitching with excitement. "New allies? Who?"

Victoria smirked. "More like *what*."

Fyrn leaned on his staff. "We are in possession of a powerful artifact and relic combination which will take the brunt of Luak's assault."

Angelique laughed humorlessly. "What artifact could

possibly be powerful enough to take the brunt of a massive army's attack?"

Victoria chuckled. "Haven't you learned yet that I'm full of surprises?"

Angelique tilted her head in annoyance, and even Audrey understood that gesture. *Just tell me.*

Audrey had to agree. Victoria was certainly milking this. From the satisfied smile on her face, though, it was clear she had gone through a hell of a lot of trouble to get this mysterious artifact.

In that moment, something in the back of Audrey's mind clicked into place.

"The golems," she said under her breath.

Most of the heads in the room turned toward her, and Fyrn let out an aggravated huff. After all, she wasn't supposed to so much as mention his pet project.

But Victoria nodded. "We have golems on our side. Golems who obey *me.*"

The room erupted into chatter as politicians and generals argued. Audrey wasn't sure why they were bothering to argue, and couldn't even catch what most of them were saying.

"Shut up!" she shouted.

Several mouths clicked shut, and a few straggling conversations died shortly thereafter.

One of the politicians along the wall—an elf who rarely spoke and whose name Audrey hadn't bothered to learn—rubbed his neck in frustration. "Golems? Are you insane? You've already gotten a third Rhazdon Artifact, Victoria. All this power, and—"

"All this power and *what?*" Diesel snapped, glaring at the elf like a man about to tear someone apart.

The elf hesitated for only a moment. "Golems are legendary for their brutality, and they obey no one. Wizards have chased them for years to *remove* the relics that power them, not bring them to life!"

Audrey lifted one surprised brow and tilted her head toward Fyrn, and the old wizard met her eye and shrugged unapologetically. Ah, so that was where he had gotten them.

"Do you see any golems breaking down buildings?" Victoria asked calmly.

"N-no."

"Do you hear any screams?"

"No."

"Are there golems ripping our armies apart?"

The elf only glared in answer.

"No," she answered for him. "They obey me. They will listen. And thanks to their indestructible bodies and sheer rage, they will save hundreds of lives in our fight with Luak. Would you rather send a lifeless rock monster onto the front lines, or your friends?"

The elf crossed his arms and stared at the floor, defeated.

Audrey reclined against the wall with a grin on her lips as she watched her friend kick ass and take names. Victoria scanned every face in the room and most met her gaze, and a few nodded to her in respect. When Victoria locked eyes with Audrey, Audrey winked once. It was their signal for, *Keep going, badass. You got this.*

"Lady Spry, do you still have access to the castle?"

"I do," the woman said as she stared at the map. Her almost vacant expression made her seem hollow—wounded, like she had seen something truly horrifying.

Living in Luak's castle, that was likely the case.

Victoria's voice softened. "After this battle, he will never harm you again."

"It's not me I'm worried about," the senator said, her voice dark. She sniffled once as she tapped a location on the map, though from this angle Audrey couldn't see what she was indicating. "I'll be here, in the heart of the castle."

Victoria nodded, taking the cue to move on. "We won't be able to reach you until after the fight is over. Can you secure yourself and keep any guards who might come for you at bay?"

The woman nodded. "The castle will lock this area off. I will be able to monitor the fight using the magic portals in this control center, so I will be able to see what's happening. I will lower the defenses once I see Luak die."

"Good," Victoria said. "Queen Angelique, your armies will divide into three sections and attack from here, here, and here." She pointed to areas on the map Audrey couldn't see.

It didn't matter. Audrey would be with Victoria to make sure she didn't die. That was all she cared to know.

The generals of each army discussed strategy for the next hour and Audrey tried her best to pay attention, but battle strategy just wasn't her thing. She didn't care about funneling troops through this, that or the other to get the optimal leverage. Maybe she should, but she didn't.

After what felt like ages, Victoria leaned back and stretched. "I think we have a plan."

The others nodded, even that elf who had protested the golems. Once he heard Victoria's plan, he had relaxed.

Victoria clapped her hands once to close the meeting. "We march tonight. We'll catch him off-guard as he goes to sleep. Make sure your people are ready, and begin moving out. The onslaught begins with my signal."

One by one the leaders funneled past Victoria, patting her on the shoulder or back as they left. They all murmured something to her as they did, and she smiled or nodded respectfully each time. Finally only she, Diesel, Fyrn, and Audrey were left.

"Never thought you'd lead a war, huh?" Audrey asked when the room was quiet again.

"Nope," Victoria admitted with a chuckle.

"Well, I'm with you to the end," Audrey said, lifting her fist.

Victoria smiled and bumped it with her own.

"As am I," Diesel said, offering his fist as well.

Audrey and Victoria grinned, bumping it in unison. The three of them turned toward Fyrn expectantly, and the grumpy old wizard rolled his eyes.

"Very well, you sentimental fools," he groaned, raising his hand.

CHAPTER TWENTY-FOUR

Victoria sat on a cliff-dwelling's balcony as she watched a dozen fires in the refugee camp flicker and burn. Far below her silhouettes huddled around them, leaning together and whispering.

The hundreds who had gathered to aid Fairhaven huddled now in silence, everyone watching the flames before they moved out in less than an hour.

Nervous energy hung in the air like fog, weighing everyone down. Ogres and elves and witches and wizards alike were afraid. She had passed a few open doors on the way up here, and had seen that even the generals and leaders sat in their rooms, watching the seconds tick by.

Deep in her core, she knew this wouldn't work. If they went into the war afraid, then…

A vision flashed in her mind of swords through stomachs, of blood, of a grinning and triumphant Luak as buildings toppled and fires raged.

Failure.

As she snapped back to the present moment, her heart

thudded in her chest. Her blood froze with panic, and she could barely breathe.

No, after everything they had done—after everything she had sacrificed—they couldn't *lose*.

It had to be the fear. The reservation. The unspoken worry that a scraggly bunch of refugees weren't enough to win a war.

They needed *hope*. If they had hope, then…

A vision flashed in her mind again of blood and carnage. A building crashed into the street, smoke billowing from its sunken roof. Screams filled her head.

But this time the figures in Luak's black mercenary uniforms ran away. This time, Luak's smile faltered, and a sword pierced his heart.

Victory.

Victoria stood on the rooftop, her heart racing as she tried desperately to think of what to do. She had to rally them. She had to inspire them, to make it known that their fear could destroy them and everything they loved.

She raced down the steps, brain buzzing with ideas. In no time at all she stood in the street, surrounded by the soldiers who were going to war under her banner. Some of these people were going to war for her—namely, the witches and wizards who had been freed in Lochrose. They felt they owed her a debt.

They owed her nothing.

"Everyone?" she shouted as loudly as she could.

Heads turned toward her as she circled the street, doing her best to get their attention. Many of the ogres lumbered closer, the ground shaking with their steps. Witches set their wands down, and several elves paused in sharpening their swords to study her face.

Truth be told, she had no idea what to say. She had never given a speech before, and definitely not to an audience this large or frightened. She didn't even know what the outcome should be beyond inspiring them. Somehow, some way, she had to take their fear and transform it into hope.

Well, perhaps she should begin with the truth.

"I know you're scared," she said. "I am, too."

A few elves close to her murmured to each other, looks of panic on their faces. Apparently *they* should be scared, but she had to be their fearless leader.

Maybe not the best start.

She pressed on. "Luak is frightening, and you have every right to fear him. I first met Luak when he killed my father in front of me and burned my house to the ground. He thrives on destruction, chaos, and yes, fear. He wants you to shake when you hear his name. He wants you to think overthrowing him is impossible."

Edgar appeared in the crowd with a large box and set it beside her with a smile.

She nodded in thanks and stood on it, doing her best to project her voice as far as possible to the gathering crowds. "But you know what? *He's afraid, too.* He's afraid of *me.* He's afraid of *you.* He's afraid of what will happen when the good people of Fairhaven and their allies have had enough! He's afraid you will burn the world around him because, my friends, you *will.*"

A cheer came from the crowd, and for the first time in her speech she saw several smiles. A few witches lifted their wands to the ceiling, sparks shooting from the tips. Elves lifted their swords and hollered in agreement.

She pumped one fist in the air, lost in her speech as she spilled her soul to any who would listen. "If you feel fear tonight, remember that Luak is terrified of your power and what you can do together! Remember why you're here! We're liberating Fairhaven from a monster. We're here to do what's right, to bring justice to the people who have been trapped in their homes or forced to run from the only life they've known. We're here to fight for those who are living in fear, unable to escape. This isn't about fear or facing death. This is about justice, honor, and sacrifice!"

The crowd cheered loudly. More swords were raised, and more wands sparked.

"And, my fellow fighters," she continued, "we have immense power on our side! To the witches and wizards of Lochrose, thank you for being here, for coming to our aid. You are heroes."

Cheers and shouts rolled out of the crowd around her, and several witches and wizards shook beneath the hearty back slaps and hugs from the ogres and elves around them.

"We have incredible power on our side," Victoria added with a mischievous grin. "Not only are we fighting beside the legendary power of Lochrose, but we also have a secret weapon Luak cannot defeat. You will see it for yourself soon. Luak does not stand a chance, my friends, and we do not need anyone else to defeat him. Those gathered here—you are more than enough. Your names will be immortalized in history as the heroes who liberated an empire, and future generations will be grateful to you!"

The crowd screamed her name.

"For justice!" she yelled over the roar. "For freedom! For *FAIRHAVEN!*"

The crowd's cheers were like thunder. Swords clashed, and overhead fireworks whizzed from hundreds of raised wands.

Fear no longer ruled in Fairhaven. With this final battle, hope would overcome.

CHAPTER TWENTY-FIVE

Audrey tensed at the mouth of a cave, peering out onto a quiet street in Fairhaven. Three of the nearby homes had been burned, and the cobblestone road led into the city's heart. In the distance, the castle's spires rose toward the immense crystal that grew from the cavern's ceiling. The dim glow of evening cast long shadows on the ground.

Hopefully Luak was asleep somewhere in that palace, because Audrey wanted to be the one to rudely awaken him.

The nervous jitters of impending battle propelled her forward, sending her in a silent run to the first building. She knelt beside it, taking cover in case a patrol should come near.

Victoria followed her, with Diesel and Fyrn hot on her heels. Beside her, Victoria closed her eyes and took a deep breath. The golden amulet in her right palm glowed like a tiny green sun as she summoned the golems.

Audrey held her breath.

The ground rumbled, and she gripped the side of the building for balance. Three perfectly round balls of rock, each twenty feet in diameter, rolled out of the massive tunnel entrance. They proceeded on command down the street, knocking over the occasional mailbox on the way.

"Let's go," Victoria said, chasing after them.

Around the city Victoria's other golems were rolling toward the castle. It would be surrounded, and while Luak tried to figure out what was going on Victoria and her armies would get as close as they needed to.

Audrey clutched the Atlantean crystal in her pocket. Time to start a war.

Angelique pressed against a building, and her warriors followed suit. Their guide, a local elf with beautiful blond hair, lifted one hand in a gesture that meant, *Wait.* He tensed, eyes scanning the darkness.

The ground rumbled, and moments later four massive balls of rock tumbled by on the way to the magnificent palace in the city center.

Her elvish guide gestured for them to continue, and Angelique followed his thin frame. After a lifetime with only witches and wizards to keep her company, the elves she met in Fairhaven were exotic and intoxicatingly beautiful. Honestly, she had never thought men could be so pretty.

It was a little distracting.

The guide led them once more into the darkness as the massive golems rolled toward the castle. The elf would take them through the streets, always ensuring they had cover on their way to the main staging area.

Angelique marveled at the golems, a smile playing at her lips as she fantasized about how they would do in battle. From all she had heard, these were powerful behemoths that would destroy everything in their paths.

She couldn't wait to see them in action.

Regina Spry stole through the castle's dark halls, her heart thudding with the surreal realization that tonight's battle would either liberate Fairhaven or damn it.

This was the end, and she had survived thus far.

When she reached the hidden door to the castle's defense system, she pressed herself against the cold wall and did her best to calm her racing nerves.

Now or never.

She knocked on the wall, and prepared to launch into her best impression of a helpless damsel. After a bit of research, she had discovered the two new guards in the tower would be harder to dupe. These elves were torturers who enjoyed the pain and suffering of others, and assigning them guard duty had been a panicked move on Luak's part.

He wanted guarantees that no one would engage the castle's defenses.

When the door didn't open, she smacked her hand against the wall again. Voice as breathless as possible, she added a shrill edge for effect. "Argo! Abson! You must help King Luak!"

She hated to use Luak's stolen title, but she had to lie to convince these morons to open this stupid door.

This time the secret passageway slid open to a scowling face. His eyes wandered her body. "What is it, woman?"

"Oh, thank goodness," she breathed, as though delighted to see the atrocious face with the massive scar over its mouth. "Luak has been attacked in his bedroom! I barely escaped, and you're the nearest guards. You must help him!"

"How convenient," a second voice said. Another elf sat in a chair by the golden portal, arms behind his head as he lazily reclined.

"Whatever do you mean?" she asked, stretching her breathless voice as much as she could.

The elf sneered. "Suspicious enchanted boulders are rolling toward the castle, and our king happens to be attacked in his charmed and secure bedroom?"

"It seems more like a setup than a rescue," the first elf said with a wicked grin.

Fine.

Regina dropped the breathless act and smirked. "You're quite right, gentlemen. Now, goodbye."

"What—"

In an instant, the chair fell through the floor as a secret trapdoor opened in the stone. The elf screamed the whole way down, and Regina didn't care to know what would become of him.

The first elf grabbed her sleeve seconds before a second door opened on the far wall. Vines wrapped around him, yanking him with unholy power into the darkness beyond.

As he was dragged into the abyss, his grip on her gown tightened. The threads ripped and Regina lost her balance.

One of the vines smacked his hand sharply, causing him to release his grip on her as they retreated. She leaned against the wall, heart pounding, as the second door slid shut, cutting off his screams.

A new chair appeared in the hole in the floor, sealing off the trapdoor once more.

"Hello, my darling Lady Spry," the castle's voice boomed.

She smiled warmly. "Hello, Fairhaven. Shall we get to work?"

"Absolutely," the mask said with a wide grin. "Let's wreak some havoc, my dear."

CHAPTER TWENTY-SIX

Victoria waited with bated breath.

With a low rumble, the final golem rolled into place. As it settled, silence crashed over the streets. The tightly curled balls of rock now encircled the palace, evenly spaced every twenty feet or so. Luak's mercenaries flooded the roads, swords drawn as they nervously studied the strange orbs.

Victoria waited alone in the shadows in an alley nearby. Audrey and Diesel had snuck over to the nearest two golems, while Fyrn had found high ground from which to cast his spells.

But she waited in the alley, back pressed to the brick wall and her full attention focused on the king's balcony. It had been King Bornt's favorite place from which to observe his people from a safe distance, and Luak would likely use it as well. It offered a secure view of the street below, and he wouldn't have to get his hands dirty.

A few of the guards began to prod the rocks,

murmuring among themselves. Apparently no one here had seen golems before.

Thank goodness! Surprise was still on their side.

"Come on," she muttered quietly under her breath, eyes still zeroed in on the balcony.

After a few moments, the doors swung open and a frustrated Luak strode onto the platform. He grabbed the railing and glowered down at the streets.

Victoria smirked. *Finally.*

"Luak!" she shouted.

She strode into the street, and the soldiers around her backed slowly away. To her relief, they watched her with fear. She had expected as much after seeing their faces in her last fight with Luak, but it had still been a risk.

But she had to lure Luak into the open.

Luak chuckled darkly. "One little warrior all by herself. Have the others grown bored with you?"

She smirked. "Not quite."

With a mighty leap, she jumped onto the nearest golem sphere and snapped her fingers. The ground rumbled beneath her as the golems came to life, slowing standing at her silent command. Her golem stretched, the smooth surface beneath her feet unfurling until she stood on its shoulders. It rose into the air, towering over the soldiers below, and she stood at eye level with the Light Elf she so dearly hated.

His arrogant smile fell and he stepped backward, jaw dropping as the golems surrounded the castle. The uncertainty on his face had been well worth the wait.

"Attack!" Victoria yelled.

Audrey held onto her golem's ear as all hell broke loose around her.

Spells whizzed through the air, streaks of blue and green and red like fireworks that ended in screams. Her golem acted on Victoria's command and carried Audrey toward the palace, where its fist connected with the wall and crashed through the stone.

Lady Spry had assured them that the witches and wizards could magic the rubble together again, but it still stung to destroy something so beautiful.

Audrey gripped her Atlantean crystal, balancing it in the hand that held the golem's ear for balance, and aimed at the mercenaries surging around the golem's feet. Several ogres rammed into its ankles, trying to knock it over.

Not today.

With the full strength of her Atlantean power, Audrey cast a thick bolt of white energy at the golem's feet. Screams followed, and several ogres in Luak's black military garb fell flat on their backs.

Heart thumping, adrenaline racing, Audrey steeled herself for the battle. This would not be easy, but not a single person in Victoria's army would surrender.

Their choices were win or die, and Audrey planned on winning.

In the castle's defense room, Regina Spry cast spells left

and right in an effort to stay on top of the utter chaos within the palace walls.

"A gaggle of roughly sixty elves are battering the east exit with their magic," the palace said calmly.

"How long can you hold them off?"

"My dear, nothing can stop me. The enchantments on my walls will keep them at bay."

She nodded, grateful the castle knew its own power so well. She had mended it from time to time, sure, but she didn't know its abilities as intimately as the king would have. "Route them south."

"I will send them through the endless tunnel. They'll run forever, thinking they're almost there the entire time."

"Good, good," she said, wiping the sweat from her brow as she studied the next glimmering portal that popped into existence before her. At least forty ogres barreled into a broad set of double doors, the only ones separating them from the madness outside.

The palace chuckled. "I have seventeen sets of doors down that hall. Every time they destroy one, another will appear. Those ogres will never break through."

Regina sighed with relief. "You truly are impressive, Castle Fairhaven."

"That I am, Lady Spry."

"How many have we contained within the castle?"

"Twelve hundred are trapped in various enchanted tunnels and by doors. Another six hundred are trying to get out through other exits, but I'll head them off. Roughly a thousand escaped into the streets."

"The rebels outside are still outnumbered," she said, grimacing.

"Oh, what do we have here?" A portal appeared before her of the royal balcony, where Luak stood with a drawn sword and circled Victoria.

"It seems we have the beginning of the end," Regina said softly, more to herself than to answer the castle's question.

The castle chuckled. "My dear, I always thought I had too much of a flair for the dramatic, but you put me to shame."

Regina shook her head, the tip of her wand glowing as she zoomed in on the fight between Victoria and Luak. "We have to help her."

"Considering where they are, I can't do much. Not many defenses were set up in that area. A poisoned arrow here, an enchanted saw there. Nothing Luak can't overcome, and they might hit the girl. That's my future queen?"

"It is," Lady Spry said breathlessly. "She just doesn't know it yet."

CHAPTER TWENTY-SEVEN

Victoria swung her sword, her magical shield in her left hand. Luak brought his blade down hard at her head, but she lifted the shield and blocked him effortlessly.

Once again she faced off with the elf who had the one thing she wanted in all the world, which was Fairhaven.

Once again she faced off with the elf who wanted to rip the powerful Rhazdon Artifacts from her dead body.

Their swords clashed as he tested her, and with every blow his immense strength challenged hers. With every grunt, every huff, every groan, they came within inches of slicing each other's heads off.

They were both always a second too late, always an inch away from a fatal blow.

Finally she had matched him, but she needed more.

She had to *win*.

Time lost its meaning in their deadly waltz. Blow after blow, strike after strike, they dodged each other. Occasionally his fist connected with her jaw and sent her flying, and other times she landed a blow to his stomach or neck, knocking him to his knees.

He had power she didn't understand and magical artifacts that rivaled her own. Whereas ogres felt like they weighed nothing and no one else could shake her, Luak could throw her clear across the street.

Luak grabbed her collar, hands bunching on the fabric as he lifted her off her feet. She cursed under her breath, summoning a dagger from her Rhazdon Artifacts and swiping at his face. The tip sliced open his forehead as he threw her off the balcony.

She landed hard on the cobblestones below, a crater all that remained of the road after her fall. Taking a wheezy breath, she glared up at the balcony and stood, wiping the blood from the corner of her mouth as she waited for him to join her.

He obliged.

When he landed, he rolled to absorb the blow. The trip would have killed most creatures, but it had been obvious for quite a while that neither she nor Luak were normal.

Without giving him a second of reprieve, she summoned the largest sword she could and swung at him. She mustered everything she had, every power she had acquired over her time in Fairhaven: her blades, her shield, her strength, her sheer force of will, her cunning, her divination.

Every blow had purpose. Every breath held power.

Bit by bit, she drove him backward and he stumbled. His sword caught hers, but barely. As her fury grew, his attacks slowed. He could only parry.

She yelled with all her soul and drove the blade toward

his stomach. He gurgled, body going rigid as she pushed the sword through until the hilt was crammed into his chest.

He stared at her, eyes wide and mouth gaping, and grabbed her hands. He gurgled again, grip tightening around her wrists as she twisted the blade to drive it in further. Thin streams of blood trailed out of the corners of his mouth.

"But you're just a human," he said, voice tense and gruff.

The opponents stilled, eyes locked, and Victoria couldn't speak. She had envisioned all the things she'd say to him when she got him like this, but couldn't think of a single thing now that it was happening.

Not a word.

"This won't matter, you know," he said, choking. "She's coming. S-she's coming. Fairhaven's hers."

"Who?" The word came out more as a demand than a question. Victoria gritted her teeth as the dying man fell to his knees.

He just laughed, blood on his teeth. His body convulsed and the tip of her sword wavered on the other side of his body, and he collapsed.

As he hit the ground, a small black orb fell out of one of the rips in the back of his shirt. Metal clattered onto the cobblestone, and a black amulet in the shape of a spider with red eyes lay on the ground before her.

In her bones, Victoria knew what it was—a Rhazdon Artifact.

A gentle ringing filled Victoria's ears as she stared at the object. There were more on his body then, hidden some-where under his clothes. Her skin buzzed at the thought of all that power mere inches away. The dagger embedded in her forearm ached, the bear figurine on her abdomen shook, and the amulet in her palm burned her with its blistering heat, but still she couldn't look away.

This elf had killed her parents, and finally—*finally*—she had fulfilled her promise to avenge them.

But she felt empty.

A hand on her shoulder snapped her back to the present and she tensed, ready to strike, until she saw Fyrn's familiar face. He watched her as though she would bolt, wary and concerned, but she simply nodded in thanks.

"Call off the golems. We've won," he said.

"Stop!" she shouted to her creatures. One by one, they obeyed and became still.

Fairhaven's protectors.

A roar crashed into her then, sudden and loud. The thrilling shouts of those around her filled her ears until she was almost deafened, and the warriors near her lifted their swords in victory.

"Victoria! Victoria! Victoria!" they shouted.

She smiled, shoulders relaxing with relief. They had done it. She shot one more glance at Luak's corpse, though, and her smile faded. She nudged Fyrn. "Destroy his Rhazdon Artifacts."

Fyrn's jaw tensed, but he nodded. "Of course."

Audrey and Diesel pushed their way to the front of the throng of people. Both had blood smeared across their faces, but they smiled warmly. Victoria had never seen a more welcome sight. They raced for her, both hugging her tightly.

"I'm so glad you're okay." She let out a sudden breath of relief.

"We did it!" Audrey yelled.

"I knew we would," Victoria said, trying with all her might not to crush them as she held them close.

She summoned her sword and lifted it toward the crystal above their heads.

"We've won!" she yelled to the sky.

And the crowd roared with her.

CHAPTER TWENTY-EIGHT

Throughout the night, fires blazed amid the rubble of the castle's exterior. Music played loudly as elves, ogres, and witches alike danced around the fires, celebrating freedom with as much wine as they could drink.

Fairhaven had been liberated, and the night became the longest celebration anyone alive could remember—even Fyrn.

But the next day around noon, Victoria sat in a war room in the east tower and laughed. It was a real laugh, a full one—the kind she hadn't experienced in a while. Tears filled the corners of her eyes, and she didn't bother holding back.

It was all too ridiculous.

"You want me to be *queen?*" she asked.

The politicians and generals at the table around her nodded. Not a single one even paused to consider her question. Even Styx nodded happily from his place on the table, but then her little pet was a bit biased.

Victoria lifted one eyebrow. "But why?"

Lady Spry smiled warmly and sat back in her chair. "This has been the plan from the beginning, Victoria."

"No one told me."

"Exactly. You would have said no."

Victoria squeezed her eyes shut, pinching the bridge of her nose as she tried to catch up with the rest of them. "Obviously. I don't need to be queen. I just wanted Fairhaven to be safe."

"That's what makes you perfect for the job."

Several men and women around the table nodded and murmured in agreement.

Victoria laughed. "Do you even hear how ridiculous—"

Diesel leaned toward her, even though he was seated several chairs to her left. "Darling, the people love you. *You* led the charge. *You* killed Luak. They want no one else."

She suppressed an eye roll. If she did become queen, she would have to talk to him about how often he used pet names with her.

"So what does this mean? I stand on the balcony and do the queen-wave? Judge rose contests?"

"You're the commander of the army," Eldrin said with a chuckle.

"You make or adjust the laws," Lady Spry added.

"You rule with compassion and mercy," Fyrn added.

"And yes," Diesel added, "you judge rose contests on occasion."

A few in the room chuckled, but Victoria stared at the table. It was all so much, so suddenly. Only yesterday…

Fyrn put an arm around her shoulder, and she looked up at her mentor. "Victoria, do you love Fairhaven?"

"With all my heart."

"Luak was working for someone, and he said this woman is coming for us. You heard his threat yourself. Do you still want to protect these people? Do you still want to protect Fairhaven, even if something worse than Luak comes for us?"

"Of course."

"Then accept. You are more suited for this role than you're giving yourself credit for."

She sighed in defeat, glancing around the room to gauge the expressions on everyone's faces. Even Audrey seemed to be in on the plan, and she winked as Victoria caught her eye.

"If that's what you want," Victoria said.

Lady Spry clapped her hands and stood. "Marvelous. Everyone, I need a moment with our new queen."

Chairs scraped the floor as most of the people stood, though Fyrn, Diesel, and Audrey remained seated. As the door shut behind them, Lady Spry's smile widened.

"I'm so grateful you accepted," the senator said.

"The monarchy hasn't been offered up quite yet, Lady Spry," a booming voice said.

Victoria stood, summoning her sword as she glared around the empty room. She balled one hand into a fist, ready to summon her shield to protect her friends. "Get down, guys! Under the table!"

Lady Spry chuckled. "Castle Fairhaven, you startled her."

Victoria lifted an eyebrow. "That was the castle?"

A golden pool appeared in the air above the middle of the table. It shimmered and swirled like ink in a lake, but Victoria didn't lower her guard. In the midst of the swirling gold a smooth face appeared, one that lacked nose or eyes. The mouth was more of a hole.

It looked like a talking mask floating in a molten pool.

"What the…" Victoria took a cautious step back, not quite processing whatever this was.

"Skeptical. Good, good," the mask said as it studied her.

Victoria snorted. "Skeptical is an understatement, buddy."

"Let's have a look at you," the mask said. In the wall behind her two of the stone blocks disappeared, and Fyrn stepped out of the way as two green vines shot from the holes. The tips lifted her hair, turned her around, and even popped open her mouth to have a look at her teeth.

She swatted at them, but they were too damn fast. "Will you stop it?"

"Hmm," the castle said to itself.

"What exactly is this accomplishing?" Victoria snapped.

"Victoria, hush," Lady Spry said quietly.

"Don't you tell me to—"

"And fiery, good," the castle said.

Victoria frowned. "Look you—"

"I'm satisfied," the castle interrupted. He nodded once, and the vines disappeared back into the wall. "You were right, Lady Spry. She is perfect."

The senator smiled. "I know."

One day later, Victoria walked down the aisle in the palace throne room in an ornate gown. The room was filled with warriors and friends, as the good people of Fairhaven and their close allies from Lochrose all crammed into the hall to see her crowned.

Freaking *queen.* She couldn't believe it, but if it put her in a position to keep Fairhaven safe she would unbegrudgingly judge a few rose contests.

Music swelled in the grand space, and the sweet aroma of lavender wafted through the air as she reached the platform at the end of the hall. The dress lifted itself as she ascended the steps, never under her heels, and she turned to face her people before sitting on the throne.

Her throne.

She straightened her back, astounded and grateful. Everything she had faced—the blood, the pain, the sacrifice—had been worth it, to see Fairhaven finally freed.

From her place beside her, Lady Spry lowered an ornate golden crown onto her head. Beams of light shot through the windows, filling the hall with an otherworldly glow. Dots of light danced on the ground as the light refracted off the stones on her head, and the crowd cheered.

Victoria couldn't help but smile broadly. Luak had taken everything from her, but she had rebuilt from the ashes. And no one—absolutely *no one*—would ever take her home and family from her again.

CHAPTER TWENTY-NINE

Victoria's first royal decree had been to restart the Berserk championships.

Hey, a girl had to have her priorities.

She sat in the royal box with Fyrn on one side and Diesel behind her. Styx waved his tiny hands in the air from his perch on the edge of the box, hooting and hollering and chattering in his gibberish language.

Angelique cheered too, but the sound cut off as she winced sharply. An ogre had just knocked an elf flat on his back, and his arm now bent the wrong way. "What a brutal sport!"

"Amazing, isn't it?" Victoria said with a chuckle. She stood and yelled at the top of her lungs. "Destroy him!"

In Victoria's peripheral view, Angelique leaned toward Diesel. "She certainly gets into it, doesn't she?"

Victoria shrugged and sat back down. "I can't help it."

Diesel laughed. "A queen can't show favoritism, my love."

"But that's half the fun! Audrey, you've got my back on

this, right?" No one answered. Victoria tilted her head, looking for her friend. "Where did she go?"

Diesel gestured to the grass below. "Down to the field. The Plits are up next."

"What? I have to get ready! Why did no one tell me?"

"Victoria," Fyrn said sternly. "You can't play."

"Like hell I can't play."

The old wizard huffed. "I already went over this with Audrey. Certainly you have a little more sense than this, girl. You're the queen. I hate agreeing with that infatuated idiot of yours, but he's right. You can't show favoritism."

"Hey!" Diesel snapped.

"Besides, it would hardly be a fair game with you on the field."

"But—"

"Game!" the announcer called from the field below.

The remaining three players—the last to not tap out despite their limps and broken arms—smacked each other on the backs and limped in unison off the field.

"Next we have the Plits versus the Snarxes!" the announcer shouted.

Below, nineteen players rushed onto the field from opposite directions, and Victoria watched with a widening smile as Audrey waved at her. Seconds later, Edgar and the remaining team members followed suit. The nine of them huddled at the end of the field, leaving her spot empty in solidarity.

They wanted her to play too.

"Screw this," she said, lifting the crown off her head and setting in gently on her chair.

Fyrn groaned. "Victoria, what—"

"I'm the queen, Fyrn. I can do whatever the hell I want."

With that, Victoria jumped from the box and braced herself for impact with the field. She landed hard in the dirt, her enhanced strength leaving her unfazed. The crowd roared as she took her place beside Audrey, who winked.

"I knew you wouldn't leave us hanging."

"Never," Victoria said, grinning. "Now let's play some Berserk!"

THE END

Get sneak peeks, exclusive giveaways, behind the scenes content, and more.
PLUS you'll be notified of special **one day only fan pricing** on new releases.

Sign up today to get free stories.

CLICK HERE

or visit: https://marthacarr.com/read-free-stories/

If smart phones and GPS rule the world - why am I hunting a magic compass to save the planet?

Austin Detective Maggie Parker has seen some weird things in her day, but finding a surly gnome rooting through her garage beats all.

Her world is about to be turned upside down in a frantic search for 4 Elementals.

Each one has an artifact that can keep the Earth humming along, but they need her to unite them first.

Unless the forces against her get there first.

AVAILABLE ON AMAZON AND IN KINDLE UNLIMITED!

For Hire: Teachers for special school in Virginia countryside.

Must be able to handle teenagers with special abilities.

Cannot be afraid to discipline werewolves, wizards, elves and other assorted hormonal teens.

Apply at the School of Necessary Magic.

AVAILABLE AT AMAZON RETAILERS

Nightfall is the last new book of 2017 for the Oriceran Universe and our 21st original title (plus two holiday shorts) by six different authors, myself included. All of those books were released in five months that went by in a blur! What a year it's been… That is a tremendous accomplishment especially when I also think about how many of those books have been on the bestseller list on Amazon and how many FANS have reached out to us to say what a good time they're having right alongside us. What an amazing thing Michael and I have created.

But… we didn't do it alone. Far from it.

We were joined by Sarah Noffke, A.L. Knorr and Flint Maxwell in this adventure. There's even a rumor that Michael Anderle will be joining the fray with a series all his own… Stay tuned for that one.

And behind the scenes are a lot of people who take care of a lot of details so that the authors don't have to or maybe we wouldn't even think to do it. There's the grand master behind the curtain, Stephen Campbell who takes care of so much that if he goes, we may have to turn off the lights and call it a day. There's his lovely wife, Julie who creates a lot of those mugs for us that we give away on release days. There's Jami Crumpton who posts all the snippets and Sarah Boyce who does the newsletter and manages the website. There's the Just in Time readers who catch more typos and gotchas (I think I hold the record for typos…) so that you guys never have to see them. There's even new people joining us with new ideas about how we can do things that you'll be hearing about in coming months. A lot of cool stuff.

And then… there's all of you. THE FANS! Over a thousand fans have joined us on the Facebook page, and over 300 have joined the Fan Group on Facebook. (If you haven't, come join us – there's a party going on in there!). All the hard work and long hours and figuring out how to make something work when a snafu hits at the 11th hour… it all goes away when we hear from you in the Amazon reviews and on Facebook and in emails how much our stories of magic and Elves and underground worlds (and that troll) add to your lives. Your enthusiasm and the way you've taken all the characters in and chat about them have made this one of the best years of my life… and we're just getting started! So, let's raise a Dr. Pepper and a handful of Cheetos and march on into 2018 and see what trouble we can raise! Aloha Everyone… More adventures to follow. A lot more.

Woop!

Book four and the end of an arc! I hope you are excited about Fairhaven, and are loving the Oriceran ride so far in 2017.

Now, I'm going to take a moment and announce that *I'm* going to be starting my own series in Oriceran in 2018.

The series title is *The Unbelievable Mr. Brownstone* (**Now available through Amazon and in Kindle Unlimited**) and I have already written the short, short prelude for my character, his ward (a teenage girl he didn't ever know he wanted to take care of... and still doesn't) and his new friends.

He didn't want those *(the friends)*, either.

He's a guy with a good heart, an ugly face (and a dog that loves him anyway), and a desire to do his job, get paid the bounty and go home.

On a planet called Earth where he wasn't even born.

Hell, for that matter, he wasn't born on Oriceran either, but Earth is the better of the two and frankly, he doesn't care to take a chance getting caught in that nasty in-between.

Some days, it just doesn't pay to get out of bed. For Mr. Brownstone, the world is a better place because he did.

It's just how he rolls.

I look forward to introducing you to Mr. Brownstone and his friends in the next few months!

Happy New Year and I hope you have a FANTASTIC 2018!

Ad Aeternitatem,
Michael

BOOKS BY MICHAEL ANDERLE

For a complete list of books by Michael Anderle, please visit

www.lmbpn.com/ma-books/

All LMBPN Audiobooks are Available at Audible.com and iTunes. For a complete list of audiobooks visit:

www.lmbpn.com/audible

CONNECT WITH THE AUTHORS

Martha Carr Social

Website:
http://www.marthacarr.com

Facebook:
https://www.facebook.com/groups/MarthaCarrFans/

https://www.facebook.com/terranavisuniverse/

Michael Anderle Social

Michael Anderle Social
Website:
http://www.lmbpn.com

Email List:
http://lmbpn.com/email/

Facebook
https://www.facebook.com/TheKurtherianGambitBooks/